The REPRESENTATIVE

Copyright 2014 by Matt Minor

dead tree
2309 Remuda Tr
Austin, TX 78745

Library of Congress Cataloging in Publication Data

Minor, Matt
ISBN 978-0-9906120-1-8

1. Texas Politics—Political Fiction 2. Texas—Culture—Fiction 3. Political Suspense
        FIC Min   PS642 M86 2014

Cover Design by: Rebecca Byrd Bretz
Author photo by Stacy Minor
Edited by: Mindy Reed, The Authors' Assistant
Formatted by: Danielle H. Acee, The Authors' Assistant

For Pablo,
who was one cool cat.

The REpRESENtATIVE

a novel by

Matt Minor

dead tree

Then, drop by caustic drop, a perfect cry
Shall string some constant harmony,
Relentless caper for all those who step
The legend of their youth into the noon.
-Hart Crane

I said all hope was vain but love...thou lovest...
-Shelley

chapter one

I.

The high definition screen illuminated perfectly the charred remnants of a little arm swinging like a metronome from a blackened bus window. The pressure from the extinguishing hose rocked the crowded, formerly yellow vehicle. Firemen raced about in the background through a thinning film of smoke. In the foreground, a network reporter spoke into a trembling microphone, repeating the same two lines: "Who could do such a thing?" And, "The sky reeks of burning tires!"

State Senator Reed Jackson stood very close to the suspended television, turning his good ear slightly upward. The volume was down very low so as not to disturb his wife Jill, who slept in the hospital bed behind him.

When the breaking news flash finished, he clicked the apparatus off. For some moments he sat staring at the blob

1

that was now his beloved wife of fifty years. Reed thought it cruel that one so emaciated could possess such little shape. *But this is cancer,* he reconciled. For the aged state senator, all was part of God's plan. There was reason for everything. *We are not meant to understand.* He felt his cell phone vibrating from the pocket of his black suit. He stepped quietly out of the room to take the call.

"Yes Governor, what is it?"

"Reed, my God, have you been watching the news! Have you heard what has just happened down in McAllen?"

"Yes sir, I was just watching; despicable."

"What kind of a sick son-of-a-bitch would blow up a school bus filled with elementary school children?"

"If I had to guess, I would say it was the cartels, sir. The Gulf Cartel to be exact."

"But why?

"The federal amnesty law paved the way for legitimate trafficking. The cartels now have legal competition. This was most likely done to deter that competition, and will no doubt be persuasive. I doubt any church groups or do-gooder organizations will venture into this area; not after this."

"What can we do?"

"Ever since the federal amnesty bill became law some months back, I've been thinking about just that. I suggest you call for a Select Joint Committee on Immigration Reform to address the immigration issue. We will need it to be a mixture of republican and democrat; it must be bi-partisan."

"Do you think the Dems will play along?"

"The general election is in less than two weeks. Everyone who voiced his or her support for amnesty will be running for the exit, sir. This is Texas' 911. To answer your question, yes, I believe the Dems will play along."

"Speaking of the general, it looks like Harry is going to get clobbered. Did you have any idea he was involved in those things?"

"Harry has the personality of an addict. Years ago I cured him of one addiction. I suppose his great flaw is that he is in need of a vice. But no, of course I had no idea. This is unacceptable. I am disgusted."

"Do you have anyone in mind for the committee?" the governor asked in an attempt to reroute the discussion to less personal and more productive aims.

"This terrorist attack occurred in McAllen, along the border. That's Representative Ron Martinez's district. I will call him shortly."

"This can't wait, Reed!" the governor implored.

"I understand, but I am at the hospital right now. It will have to wait, sir."

"I'm sorry, Reed, how thoughtless of me. How is Jill?"

"She's dying, Governor."

"I'm terribly sorry Reed…terribly sorry."

"It is alright sir; soon she shall be with the Lord. I will call you tomorrow when I have something."

"God Bless you, Reed."

"God Bless Texas, sir."

When Reed reentered Jill's private room, he found that all the instruments which detailed her vital sign's had collapsed. The

EKG was flat. He kissed Jill on the forehead and then pressed the remote that alerted the nurse. A single stoic tear traveled the furrows of his face. Taking a seat near the bed, he took her hand, which was still warm. *Yes,* he thought, *now she has gone home.* He wondered when he would join her. He prayed it would not be too long. Reed was now alone on this earth: His son having died years ago in a car accident and his lesbian daughter estranged and beyond contacting. In joining Jill, he prayed it would not be long.

When the nurse arrived, he informed her of his wife's passing. Personnel came and went. Reed, having returned to the television, watched more of the unfolding devastation. He had loved God with all his heart his whole life. The Lord had repaid him with professional success, but balanced that success with personal tragedy. It had been his cross to bear. He watched as the firemen started the careful process of removing tiny bodies from the explosion; knowing he had one more cross to bear before he joined his wife in eternity.

II.

Though the rain had subsided, the weather now took a turn for the worse. The dark country road shot with certainty into an increasingly confident mist. Within this fogbank traveled someone wholly uncertain.

"Damn it, where is it?" Tryphena mumbled tensely, as her right hand blindly sifted through her purse, which sat in the passenger's seat. Having located her cell phone, she then began the dangerous process of dialing the proper contact. The car, a Mustang nearly ten-years-old, had slowed to a glorified roll. The brights were promptly switched on.

"Answer, please answer," she pleaded, as a fragmented ring became audible in her ear.

"Hello?" A deep voice asked, cutting in and out.

"Warren?"

"Yes."

"This is Tryphena! Can you hear me?"

"Tryphena! Yes, I can hear you, but not very well. Already done with the interview? How did it go?"

"It didn't go, not yet. I'm not there yet."

"What! Why not? It's after eight!"

"Warren, I'm lost! I have no idea where I'm at! The road has vanished. There are no streetlights. I don't know what to do!"

"OK, calm down. Are you following your GPS? Why has the road vanished?"

"Warren, I don't have GPS." While this conversation dragged on in confused frustration, a neon smudge appeared through the numerous running cracks of the Mustang's front windshield.

A neon 'PECK'S BARBECUE,' gradually took form. "I'm here; oh my God!" Tryphena shouted, slamming on her brakes.

"You've found it?"

"Yes, yes! I'll call you back." She hung up and pulled the Mustang off the road. Gravel popped under the worn tires.

The young woman, freshly graduated from college, let go a deep sigh, opened her car door and stepped into the dank November night.

"God, I hope he won," she muttered to herself. "Jesus Christ," she nervously complained as her dark blue pumps struggled across the rocky parking lot.

Tryphena was late, very late, nearly an hour. As she walked towards the entrance of Peck's Barbecue, her head swam with doubt. *What kind of Democrat has a victory party at a hick BBQ place? I bet this place is all white people. They won't understand my name. I'll have to repeat it again and again.*

Country music roared as she opened the heavy wooden door. Rich meat smells hit her like a soiled diaper. The fresh graduate was correct; it looked to be all white people. She surveyed the long skinny room of littered tables and searched for the face she knew only from a shitty website, newspapers and mail advertisements. No one distinguished themselves.

"Excuse me; I'm looking for Candidate Dothan?" she asked a trashy patron who stood leering into the jukebox selection screen.

"Over there!" the woman answered, gum smacking—her nipples apparent through her white tank top. Tryphena took a deep breath, zeroed-in on the respective spot, and made her way through the tangle of tables. Dothan's short, jet-black hair caught her radar, although his back was turned to her. He sat talking diligently to a table full of white-collar men without jackets. As she approached him from behind, suddenly he turned in his chair and addressed her.

"You!" He declared, pointing his finger straight at her.

The woman was completely taken aback. She stopped in her tracks and stiffened. "What do you prefer…" he paused, "Black or African-American?"

"I really don't mind. I'm not easily offended," she answered smugly, tightly clenching her eyebrows involuntarily.

"Good answer!" Dothan replied definitively, without a hint of self-consciousness. He turned back towards the table of men and continued his discussion.

Tryphena stood, confused. *What has just happened?* But before she could get her bearings, a chubby, visibly balding man stood up from the table.

"You're Ms…." He snapped his fingers and began shaking his head up and down as if trying to jar his memory.

"Taylor," Tryphena confirmed.

"Taylor! I'm sorry, Ms. Taylor, I'm Jack Clark, Dothan's campaign manager. Your recruiter, our consultant, Warren Jenkins, told me you were coming out tonight. With all the excitement, it slipped my mind. Please forgive me. Please, take a seat."

Tryphena took the only available seat, the one directly across from the candidate. "Ms. Taylor, to your right is Mitch Stevens from the *Herald*; left, yours truly; and sitting across from you, the next State Representative for House District 100, John David Dothan!"

"There are still too many precincts out to say that officially, Clark. Don't jinx me now." Dothan retorted, looking straight at Tryphena.

"Pleased to meet you, Representative Dothan," she confirmed.

"Look what ya' started, Clark!"

Just then, Clark's cell phone started ringing. "It's the County

Democratic Chair!" Clark announced while vacating the table in search of a quieter locale.

"Tell me, Ms. Taylor, what is your first name?" Mitch Stevens asked.

"Tryphena."

"What?" Dothan interrupted.

"Tryphena!"

"Oh, that's pretty. Where did you go to school?"

Tryphena knew that neither one of the two men understood her name—they never did. "University of Houston."

"What in?"

"Political Science."

"JD!" Clark yelled from across the barbecue joint. "It's in— it's official—it's yours, you lucky so-and-so! You won!"

"Speech time!" Tryphena said in a sing-song tone, looking straight into Dothan's glassy black eyes.

"You want to wait for Jessica?" Stevens asked Dothan.

"No. She'll be here, at some point."

"Shouldn't we wait for Harry to call?" Dothan inquired of Clark as the campaign manager stood over their table, squeezing into his jacket like a sausage into a wrapper.

"No, we can call him back if he calls to concede while you're speaking!"

Peck's Barbecue consisted of two compartments: the long skinny dining area where the party presently sat, and a banquet hall. All activity now moved to the latter. Several local reporters fluttered about, snapping pictures. This was not an election of sufficient magnitude to warrant television. Jack Clark, sifting through the collection of supporters, mounted the small stage at the very back. It, like the dining area, was littered with animal heads, a taxidermist's dream. The floor, the walls, indeed the ceiling were covered with hunters' paraphernalia. The entire establishment looked to be carved from some giant piece of wood. In fact, a live oak rose through the center of the banquet hall—literally rising up through the floor and out the roof.

"Can I have your attention, please?" Clark requested through the microphone. "Folks, I would like to present to you our new State Representative, John David Dothan!"

As the newly elected Rep. took the stage, his newly hired aid listened from the banquet hall entryway. But was she hired? *How informal could this be?* Tryphena pondered. From the corner of her eye a group of country black folk entered the dining area. *Are they a part of the party?* she wondered.

Dothan's speech was well delivered. Only, he sounded a lot like a Republican. At one point, he even defended ending ethanol subsidies, a major economic boon to the region. His logic was eloquent, however.

"In the past decade, we have seen our cotton production fall into the proverbial furnace where we now burn our corn! As a result, not just agricultural feed, but global food prices, have sky rocketed, further disenfranchising the already desperate peoples of the Third World!"

What the hell does this have to do with state government? she wondered.

Dothan continued, "Through unwise trade agreements, the Free Trade Republicans have consummated the destruction of our once formidable textile industry of the Southeastern United States. Meanwhile, the price of cotton rises!"

His summary, due to its melodrama, irritated her.

"Soon, we might find ourselves, not only unable to feed our livestock, but unable to clothe ourselves."

"That's right, brother!" A fat, elderly black man dressed in overalls bellowed from where he stood in line, waiting to order. This further irritated Tryphena, as it was a strategically dropped line meant to appeal to the emotions.

But all in all, Dothan was OK, she surmised. Even if he were not, he was going to have to suffice. Tryphena wanted a job as Chief of Staff, period. She was applying for this position at Dothan's office at the Capitol in Austin. With no experience, this was the only opening available to her. Observing his gestures, the way he moved when he spoke, it was obvious his success was due to his good looks; not that his oratory skills were not above average. But a short, chubby, ugly man, saying the same thing with the same voice would most likely not have been elected; particularly not a Democrat; not in this part of the country.

Dothan was finishing up his speech as a band began setting up behind him. The musicians were wearing cowboy hats. The newly elected signed off to overwhelming applause, yielding the microphone back to Jack Clark.

"Now, how many of y'all would like to hear JD sing a few songs?" Clark's feigned plea was given an exaggerated twang. Tryphena was over it. She pushed her way towards the front of the crowd and kindly demanded to speak with the campaign manager turned American Idol host.

"Mr. Clark, I appreciate the jubilation, but I'm curious as to the status of my employment. I did drive a long way. No one, as of yet, has interviewed me."

With the band in the middle of sound check, it made it necessary for Clark to nearly scream as he leaned down from atop the stage. "You're hired, Ms. Taylor!"

"What?"

"You…are…hired!"

"Hired? Really?"

"Yes! Welcome aboard!"

Tryphena shook hands and then subtly drifted out of the banquet hall. Dothan, now stripped not only of his jacket, but his tie as well, stood at the mic with a guitar strapped around his neck.

"I wasn't planning on doing this, but I guess…"

The roar of the small crowd overtook him. Tryphena, slipped out the front entryway and just barely escaped.

III.

Tryphena's alarm went off every morning at 5:30, except for Sunday. She rubbed the previous night's grit carefully from her youthful eyes and searched for the case to her contact lenses. A hacking cough became audible from the other side of her bedroom door.

"Rufus?" she inquired, emerging from her tiny room into the tiny den of her tiny apartment. She discovered the thin, gray-headed man in a wheelchair, leaning forward, his head hovering over the toilet.

"It's alright baby, it's alright." The man struggled to enunciate through spasms and phlegm.

"Have you called Dr. Corel?"

"That nigger don't know what he's doin'!"

"Father, I have asked you repeatedly not to use that term around me."

"I'm sorry baby, but it's true."

Tryphena smiled a fatalistic, forlorn smile. Then, squeezing into the narrow crevice that existed between her father's chair and the toilet and wall, she wheeled him into the breakfast area.

"How'd it go last night, baby?" he asked.

"I got the job," she answered from the bathroom where she stood methodically putting in her contact lenses. "Thirty-five thousand a year."

"Thirty-five thousand…my God that's more money than I ever made in my entire life. I'm so proud of you, Tryphena."

The two stood looking at one another strangely through the mirror, like the last two survivors of a shipwreck, having just washed ashore, their meager rations between them. "I'm going to the bank this afternoon. Give me your disability check and I'll deposit it."

"I already cashed it, baby."

"You already cashed it? You didn't," Tryphena scolded.

"I only spent a hundred dollars on the Lotto, baby. That's all!"

Before she could descend into interrogation, her cell phone rang.

"Where's my purse?" she asked, flustered. She found it where she did not remember leaving it and answered, "Warren?"

"Yes, hey, Tryphena, sorry to call you so early, but I talked to Jack Clark." There was a pause.

Her heart now began racing with doubt. *Did I leave too soon? That same trick I always play on myself, when I think something is in the bag; I begin to have contempt for it.* "You talked to Jack Clark…and…?"

"Well, there's a bit of a problem…"

Tiny beads of sweat appeared on her forehead. Her heart rate was accelerating. "A problem?"

Rufus reacted, turning around in his wheelchair.

"Well, first off, you left without giving them your contact information. But no biggie, they can call me. The problem is, well…"

"What is it Warren, please, just tell me!"

Rufus looked up at his daughter with a look of passive alarm.

"I know you signed on to work at the Capitol, but Dothan needs some help putting together his district office first. It's really not official until the House approves it, next month, after the swearing-in. But we want to get it going now. Do you mind going down to Matagorda and helping him get it in order? It's pretty informal; Clark said they'll write you a campaign check."

"When?"

"This afternoon if you're available."

"What's the address?"

⌇

The sun was just beginning to rise as Tryphena vacated her complex. She lived in a suburb of Houston known as Alief. Alief, like so many parts of Houston, was once a prospering area. It was now home to so many different, unassimilated nationalities as to render it dysfunctional. Her newfound job was her ticket out. Matagorda was some fifty miles away.

The fog of the previous evening still lingered. The drive was slow and dull, like the weather. The whole way down she was wracked with the anxiety so familiar to the working poor. The sense that at any moment, the balance might shift and the proverbial car plunge into the abyss.

She arrived at her destination with little difficulty. The district office was only a few hundred yards from the Gulf of Mexico, and situated in a strip center. There was no sign on the building, only a single banner hanging in the front windows. The door was open, the stopper nudged against the mildewed sidewalk. Tryphena entered. The front room was completely vacant with the exception of a few boxes.

"Hello?" she asked with just a touch of timidity—nothing, no reply. The front room collided with a short hallway. The hallway offered up several doors. "Hello?" she asked again, wondering if maybe somehow she was in the wrong place. Then, the very faint sound of music emanating from a room at the end of the hall drew her towards it. The door was partly open. She knocked and stood, waiting for a response; again nothing. She pushed the door softly open with her index finger and discovered her new employer seated at his desk. His face was concealed by an old, crinkled Tomb of Dracula comic book; headphone wires pouring out from his ears. The music he listened to did not sound like country and western.

Tryphena stood feeling awkward, wondering how to make her presence known. Perhaps a minute went by before Dothan realized that she was standing before him. He was startled as much by her sudden appearance as by her beauty, which in the chaos of last night he had failed to really take note of. He put the comic book down and removed the headphones from his ears, one at a time. "Tryphena, right?"

She was amazed that he had gotten it right—first try. This aided considerably in her judgment of him, particularly considering that she had just discovered him reading a comic.

"That's right, Representative Dothan: Tryphena Taylor."

Dothan stood, staring at her for an instant. In that instant he devoured her exquisite figure as well as her tasteful dress. Although her cloths were not expensive, Tryphena knew how to make do. Truth is, to the individual man, a woman whom he finds attractive, looks good in anything. This woman wore a long sleeve, green top. Her pants: black. The blouse broke up perfectly the black of her hair and the black of her slacks; the high cheekbones created a soft angularity—consistent from top to bottom.

"Let's find you a chair, what do ya' say?" Dothan placed the iPod down and emerged from behind his desk. The music in the headphones continued to saw. He wore blue jeans with black cowboy boots; a blue collared shirt tucked neatly in.

Tryphena could not help thinking he looked cute. "What are you listening to?" she asked.

"Oh, the Ramones. Do you like old school punk music?"

"Oh, I don't know. I'm kind of partial to old school R&B. It's what my mother used to listen to."

Dothan was as impressed with her taste as she was confused by his. "Used to; why did she stop?" he asked loudly as he went room to room looking for a chair.

"Oh, she passed away a few years ago: cancer."

"Here we go," he said, entering back into the office. After placing the chair down, he stood over it from behind, offering her a seat.

"Thank you." She sat down and became aware of the Columbia blue on the surrounding walls. It seemed to radiate a sort of cool warmth.

"So, your mother died of cancer. I'm so sorry. How old were you, if you don't mind me asking?" Dothan now resumed his previous position, seated behind his desk.

"I was twenty, sir."

"That's awful. I'm so sorry."

"It's been four years now. I've gotten somewhat used to it."

"But your father, your father is still alive?"

"Yes, he came to live with me after my mother died."

"Then he's a comfort to you, good."

"Well, I hardly knew him growing up. He was never really around. He has emphysema, now. He's kind of sick."

"My God, you must be wise, very wise beyond your years."

Tryphena was somewhat startled at that observation. Few people ever read anything significant into her personal issues. They rarely listened. She had not expected a statement so observant from a politician who hardly knew her. Although Tryphena was very politically liberal, she was not an idealist. Years of deprivation had marked her with a raw realism. She knew all too well the flaws inherent in people.

The day was productive, with Tryphena exhibiting a decorating flair unknown even to her. Box after box was emptied. When the movers arrived, they delivered more bookshelves than filing cabinets. Dothan it seemed, was a reader, and not just on politics. There were numerous books of poetry, as well.

People came and went all day: Jack Clark, Mitch Stevens, and congratulatory constituents, each with a crate of files or office-warming gift. Dothan's cell phone rang incessantly. The short day spilled over into night; Tryphena noticed one consistency above all others: there was no sign, or mention, of a 'Ms. Dothan.'"

chapter Two

The road to John David Dothan's residence wound through a grove of squatty, unkempt palm trees. The grounds beyond stretched out in a sandy flatness—broken only by weedy dunes. All that was left of a productive day was a strip of orange to the west.

Dothan killed the engine of his green, short-bed, '74 Ford pickup and gathered his things from the passenger seat. He climbed the twelve steps to the front door and set down his briefcase and beer; he hesitated. He carefully unlocked the door and pressed it open softly before bending down to retrieve his articles. The door creaked open like an out of tune, aching violin.

No one was present upon entry. The low cedar ceiling of the den reverberated with a radio playing down a hall.

"Hey there, fella!" A feminine drawl called from his flank, the kitchen.

"Hey there, gal," Dothan replied, startled.

Jessica, his wife, emerged from the shadows of the kitchen;

dressed only in her nightgown, drinking a Screwdriver. The way the light outlined her face made her look gaunt, almost old. Jessica was one of those women of middle age obsessed with matching the weight she had once had in her early twenties. As a result, her facial bones pulled too tightly at her skin. Although aloofness might, health no longer sparkled from Jessica's once supple features.

"State Representative, congrats."

"Thank you. I thought you wouldn't be back 'til tomorrow."

"I cut the vacation short. Sorry I missed the shindig. How'd it go?"

"I won. It went well."

"Daddy sends his congratulations as well, JD."

Dothan put his six-pack in the refrigerator and went searching for a bottle opener. Jessica stood on the perimeter of the light and looked her husband up and down. "It's probably in the dishwasher. That damn maid never unloads that thing."

"She needs to dispense some sort of air-freshener. It smells like the beach in here." Dothan cracked his beer open and turned around to find Jessica right behind him; her gown open, her breasts exposed.

"I've never done it with a congressman before." She now had her hand on his crotch.

"Technically, I'm not a congressman. Didn't you get enough of that this past week?"

"Whatever, 'congressman' is close enough! And oh please, you know that was just a girl's getaway. Won't you forgive me? I tried to get back in time," she teased.

"It's not like the first Tuesday in November is that hard to schedule around. They've had this thing since Ancient Rome, it's called a calendar."

"You're such a smart ass!" Jessica retorted and pulled away.

Dothan slammed his beverage down on the counter, lurched forward and grabbed Jessica's arm; thrusting her forcibly into his chest.

"Oh, you're not gonna tie me up, are you? I like it when you're rough with me."

"Is that what I have to do to get you to love me, knock you around?"

"You're such a sucker, JD."

Dothan lifted Jessica up in his arms and marched her into the quarters that were once their bedroom. He threw her down on the bed and the two proceeded to perform an act that had become a rarity in this house.

~

"You want a beer, JD?" Jessica asked from the bathroom.

"Sure."

She returned from the kitchen with the two beverages and discovered her husband sitting up in bed smoking a cigarette.

"Isn't that a bit cliché? When's the last time you checked your blood pressure?"

"This morning, it was a little high. But I had had a couple of cups of coffee." Something was eating at Dothan. A something that sex could not entirely purge.

"It was bad enough that you weren't present last night. At least you could've sent your father. There just wasn't anybody there. I was so embarrassed."

"You know Daddy always goes goose hunting this time of year. Don't go feeling sorry for yourself, JD. If those puppy dog eyebrows droop anymore it might make me want to cry."

Dothan exhaled the last of his smoke and crushed it out in the spotless ashtray beside the bed.

"You'll hear from him soon enough. You know, he's gonna expect you to go to bat for him in Austin."

"Our state's in debt Jessica; in this climate I don't know how I can justify tax breaks and subsidies that won't bring in any revenue in the short term or the long. Besides, the Republicans run this thing wholesale, for now."

"You're good at maneuvering, JD. You'll figure something out. Daddy's gonna expect a return on his investment."

Dothan sat staring into space.

Jessica could tell he wasn't listening. "Well, we can talk about it tomorrow. Do you want the light out? What time you want to get up?"

Lying alone in the dark, Dothan's mind was teeming with thought. He simply could not get to sleep. Images from the previous night, as well as from that day, filled him with a mixture of pride and anxiety. But the thought of Tryphena brought a smile to his face. What a beautiful, driven woman she appeared to be. She seemed to take nothing for granted. Juxtaposed with his wife, Jessica, she seemed almost angelic. Jessica was typical of her background: smug, indifferent, and largely uncaring. Oh, she would pontificate about this cause or that cause, but it was all abstraction. The tangible, the real, she met with almost derision. She would write a check for a thousand dollars to an animal shelter, but she could not be bothered with actually helping a stray. *Has she always been like this?* he wondered. They had known each other for nearly twenty years. *Where did the time go?* he pondered. The universality of the question belied his innate sense of isolation. For an instance, he brooded on his lack of originality. *Almost twenty years?*

JD and Jessica met when the former was twenty-four, and the latter twenty-three. Dothan, who was scratching by, living the life of a rock-n-roll singer, was larger than life to the young woman. He seemed the iconoclast incarnate. She enjoyed his petulant swagger, that insignia of passionate, vain, carefree youth. It was Austin in the nineties. Jessica was a student at the university. Life was an open book. Like her girlfriends, Jessica had become something of a groupie around Dothan's band. The other girls, less confident, less rich—sought after the other members. Jessica, however, wanted the frontman; she wanted Dothan.

Dothan was a dropout—even better. How better to piss off her controlling father than to date, not only a wannabe rock star, but also a college reject. She had first seen him perform when opening for Jesse Jackson. The activist had come to the campus to speak; Dothan's band had been chosen to warm up the crowd. JD commanded the stage. With his long curly black hair, his angular jawbone, he resembled Jim Morrison—from a distance that is. Up close, it was sadness rather than madness, which emanated from his eyes. They melted the surface of Jessica's heart. The man himself would quickly thaw what was beneath. What a time that was. But time can work on the respective heart the way it works on the world: ages of fire…ages of ice. The epoch of fire had diminished. What was now left was a frozen wasteland. Dothan had given up trying to rekindle what was now a phantom. He had become accustomed to the notion that divorce was imminent. Running for office was less a way to earn back Jessica's devotions, but rather a reassertion of the man's instincts.

~

Dothan had hardly been up for five minutes when the phone rang.

"It's Daddy."

He removed himself and his coffee into the privacy of his office; the representative elect took the call.

"Yes, sir."

"Am I to understand congratulations are in order?"

"Yes, sir, you understand correctly."

"I knew you could do it, JD. Sorry I couldn't be there for the victory party."

"No problem. I'm looking forward to some good eatin.'"

"Next year you need to come with me."

"I'm putting it on my calendar as we speak."

"I'm having my secretary fax over some new figures on the proposed Historical District in Brazoria. The figures come straight from the Chamber of Commerce. This will be a big project, bring in many jobs."

"I'm not sure if this is the climate to ask for almost twelve million in pork, sir." Dothan waited for what he knew would be a severe reproach.

"Goddamn it JD, just look over the figures and get back to me!"

"Uh, yes, sir." His resolve never sustained itself. This conversation was over.

"You know I appreciate it, JD. Put Jessica back on, will you?"

'Daddy,' was Jacob Langhorne II, son of a wildcatter turned millionaire. Although Jessica's father had no aptitude for the energy industry, he had managed to carry on the family fortune, perhaps not in the capacity of his father, but sufficiently enough. Jacob Jr. joined the contracting world in his thirties, and found his niche in the restoration industry. His life's blood was government money.

II.

Through the duration of her college years, Tryphena had worked as a waitress at an Italian restaurant not far from her apartment. The young woman, though accustomed to menial jobs, was a little embarrassed, being that she was now a college graduate. The clientele at this restaurant was diverse, like her neighborhood. The tips varied.

"So what do you say, Saturday, after work?"

"Rudy, you know I have a policy of not dating *any* coworker."

Tryphena would surrender. Rudy had what the other losers without plans lacked, charm and ambition. The charm was easily identifiable; it was the ambition that was hazy.

Saturday arrived and Tryphena was nervous. It had been some six months since she had dated a man, more than a year since she had actually slept with anyone. In her aquiline mind she had made many dating resolutions. Of late, she had resolved herself not to date African-American men ever again. They were simply incapable of responsibility. But after dating a white man who was incorrigibly lackadaisical, she concluded men as a whole were worthless. Loneliness successfully retorted with her acceptance of Rudy's advances.

While Rudy, the weekend manager, went over receipts with the cashier, Tryphena readied herself in the bathroom. She felt sick to her stomach and worried about the night ahead. *What if I have to go to the bathroom while I'm with him? What if he tries to get me back to his place? What if he tries to have sex with me? What if I concede and he doesn't want to wear protection?* Her mind was conjuring every negative possibility imaginable. She had a Xanax in her purse, given to her months ago by a girlfriend who suffered from anxiety. In a fit of haste she almost took it, but decided against the notion.

"So you're good with the pool hall, right?"

"Yes, that sounds like a plan," Tryphena replied, sitting up stiffly in the passenger seat of Rudy's car. Her stomach issues had not abated and she felt like she was on the verge of panic. Tryphena reached over and turned up the dial on the radio. "I like this song!"

"Cool!" Rudy said as he hit the accelerator.

Once inside the pool hall, Tryphena excused herself to the ladies room. *What is happening to me? Why do I feel like I'm on the verge of something terrible?* She sat on the toilet and began going through her purse. Again she struggled with whether or not to take the tranquilizer. Again she decided against it. What she did need, however, was a drink.

Tryphena rarely drank, but she reasoned this was as good an excuse as any. Neither did she know much about pool, which Rudy liked. The game gave him the opportunity to take charge, be the man. After a few glasses of wine, Tryphena's nerves settled. The night, which began anxious, was turning out to be just fine. By the time two a.m. rolled around, and it was time to go, Rudy had found that sweet spot that most women possess—the sweet spot that dismantles the barricades.

The question invariably came up, on the theoretical way home, as to the next destination. The wine was working its magic in unison with Rudy's charm. It didn't hurt that Tryphena found the man physically attractive. Rudy was very athletic. She looked over at his profile from the passenger seat and replied with a question, a riddle of sorts. The answer of which was the final click in the combination that unzipped her pants.

"So, are you going to pursue football anymore, maybe walk on at the University of Houston?"

Rudy had been the star quarterback at the high school that they both had attended. Numerous colleges had scouted him. The only bite, however, was a school in North Dakota. After one winter in the frozen northland, Rudy had had enough. Coming home, he bounced in and out of school.

"Oh, I don't know. I'll be twenty-four soon. That's kind

of old to be trying to play college ball, Tryphena." Whether or not his answer, in reality, made sense or not, was irrelevant. Rudy had failed to answer the riddle.

"We need to pick up my car at the restaurant."

"Yeah, I know," Rudy replied with a laugh meant to disguise his disappointment.

Tryphena unlocked the door to her apartment and entered into near darkness. A television flickered, illuminating a dreadful sight.

"Rufus?" she called out.

Her father was sitting in his wheelchair at the kitchen table, slouched over with his face crashed into the top of it. Tryphena hastily switched on the lights and discovered her father sitting in a small pool of blood.

"Father!" she cried, carefully lifting his head up. Rufus was unconscious; blood was caked all over his face, presumably from his nose.

"Oh my God!" Tryphena's heart was racing. Any lingering effects of the alcohol had vanished. She reached for the phone and dialed 911.

As Tryphena filled out the endless paperwork in the emergency room, her mind drifted into a curiously odd direction. She began pondering her first date with Rudy. Though not for very much longer, Rudy was her boss. *How will this affect my work environment? Maybe I was too hard on him. I'm just so sick of worthless men. But he is the manager. Someone entrusted him with a degree of responsibility. I certainly wouldn't want to do his job. The owner is a prick.* Indeed, she began to reevaluate the entire experience. She would surmise that somehow, she had blown it. Her dark musings were interrupted by the here and now.

"Ms. Taylor?" A tired looking man in a white coat asked as he stood over her.

"Yes?"

"We have your father stabilized. I understand that you found him passed out?"

"Yes, that is correct."

"Well, Ms. Taylor, your father simply passed out. His COPD is inhibiting his intake of oxygen. If it flares up, and he can't get enough air, he simply passes out. Obviously this is dangerous. But there are more serious issues at stake, as well," the doctor said, setting down the clipboard.

Tryphena, gazed forlornly at the doctor and asked despondently, "What could be more serious than not being able to breath? I mean, that will kill you."

"Yes ma'am, but what we're really concerned about is Anoxic Brain Damage; or, to a lesser degree, a slowed dementia."

"What are these?"

"If your father goes long enough without air—literally just a few minutes—it could kill a portion (or portions) of his brain. That's not what happened tonight. It wasn't that severe. If what happened tonight continues, which is the more likely scenario, he could steadily lose brain function. The symptoms of dementia resemble Alzheimer's."

"What do we do?"

"I'm going to up the dosage on his meds."

"He's on Medicaid, that doesn't cover what he takes now."

"Yes, I understand. Maybe you should talk to your...Dr. Corel, I believe is his name?" The ER doctor asked, looking at his chart.

"What's *he* going to do?"

"Perhaps he could supply your father with enough samples to at least see if it will help?"

With that piece of good cheer, the doctor excused himself.

Tryphena sat staring at the pale phosphorescent walls all around her. She felt cold, very cold. Her mind wandered back to the recent past, recalling the warmth of a certain state representative's office; the cadence of crashing waves in the background.

chapter Three

As they receded, the dirty gray waves left salt stains on John David Dothan's old gray boots. Looking out over the Gulf of Mexico, which served as his backyard, the leaden surroundings struck him profoundly. The heavily overcast sky was indistinguishable from the waters. It was almost dark out. Dothan turned toward his house and his gaze was drawn to the Christmas tree in the window. *What a peculiar time this is*, he thought. Christmas in his adult years had become an annual disappointment. Dothan tried in vain to recapture something from his youth. Only once in his adult life had he caught that "something," and that was itself a long time ago.

"Are you ready JD?" Jessica called from the balcony.

Her shout shattered his meditation. "Yes," he answered.

~

"I hope she doesn't get pissed off like she did last year."

"She might, we didn't go to see her at Thanksgiving."

"There was too much going on, Jessica."

"I know JD, but she's gone crazy!"

The two were headed to a retirement facility down the coast towards Corpus Christi. The retiree was Dothan's mother. It was after eight in the evening when the couple arrived at their hotel.

Black night oozed into gray day. JD and Jessica arrived at the rest home around 9:00 a.m. the next morning; both were hung over.

"How is she?" Dothan asked the nurse at the front desk, concerned. "Was she angry that we didn't come to see her at Thanksgiving?"

Jessica interrupted, "What he means is he won an election last month and hasn't talked to her since. She knew he was running. The question is, does she remember?"

Dothan peered over at his wife in silent disgust.

"She ain't been doing well. That's all I know," the nurse informed them.

"What, why didn't anyone contact me?"

"We did call. In fact, we called several times," the nurse, scolded.

Dothan was in no mood for a confrontation. When Jessica sent out the signal to her husband that she might be, he nudged her in the ribs with his elbow. Surprisingly she acquiesced.

As Dothan moved down the hall towards his mother's room, behind the nurse and Jessica, he could not quell that familiar swell of tears that always accompanied this instance.

"Mrs. Dothan?" the nurse asked, peering into the room.

There was no reply.

Dothan stepped into the doorway and saw the gray, straight, knotted hair of the woman who bore him. She sat in a wheelchair facing the wall. "Mother?" he asked.

"Mrs. Dothan, " Jessica interjected. "How have you been? Merry Christmas!"

"What? I know that voice," the old woman replied. She tried to turn her chair around and the nurse hurried over to assist her. "Yes, I know that voice," Mrs. Dothan declared with joy as she saw the couple standing in the entrance of her quarters.

"Hello mother."

Perplexed, the woman looked up at her son in confusion. "Mother? You must be kidding mister. I don't have a son. I only have a daughter named…Jessica. Isn't that right, dear?" She smiled and turned towards her perceived progeny.

The nurse turned her gaze to Dothan and shook her head at the tragic situation.

No, Mrs. Dothan, I'm your daughter-in-law," Jessica said, stressing the last two syllables. "This nice looking man next to me is your son, John David."

"John David? I don't know any John David."

Dothan was unable to control the muscle spasms of his face; he began to tear up.

"What are you crying for mister, are you some sort of fool or something?"

Dothan left the room abruptly.

Jessica found her husband sitting on a bench outside on the nursing home grounds. She could tell he was sobbing, however discreetly. She paused and studied his crooked figure with a sense of regret for time itself, and its ravaging effect on us all. Dothan, through sniffles and tears was gazing out at the barren yellow landscape, spiked with small trees supported by stakes and rope. *How odd a moment can be in a life,* he thought, *a line of demarcation that once drawn, divides our time into: before and after.* Before entering the room, John David Dothan was some- one's son. Now, after exiting, he was only a stranger.

Jessica had not felt much for the sordid character sitting on the bench in quite some time. But this display of quiet grief reminded her that JD was her husband and not just a series of unfulfilled longings and desires. She went over, stood behind him and put her arms around his neck. When she bent down to kiss him, Dothan began to sob uncontrollably.

"Hey, hey there fella, it's alright now. The nurse said that she goes in and out. She'll remember you here soon enough."

This was a lie. The nurse had actually informed her that she was surprised she recognized anyone. The old woman's mind was going quickly now.

"It would be better if she had just died like my father— one day—just gone. Like a drop of the guillotine. Not like this. This is monstrous, Jessica."

"I know JD. I know," she agreed as she rubbed his shoulders.

It had been a long time since the passing of Dothan's fa- ther—over a quarter century. His death meant more than just the loss of a parent; it meant the loss of a lifestyle. A well-to-do attorney, Phillip Dothan had provided his wife and only child with a fine standard of living. No need went unanswered. Few wants were denied. But a fatal heart attack ended all of that.

John David was only fifteen when his father died, abruptly. As he sat on the bench, still in his wife's embrace, he thought back upon that dreadful day—the day when he arrived home from school and found his mother, a young woman, much like Jessica now, in tears.

"I remember coming home that day. It was so nice out, so fair. It was late September."

"Yes, yes it was." Although Jessica had heard this tale before, she listened as if listening to a sad sentimental tune, while painful in the abstract, one never tires of.

"My mother was sitting in the kitchen, at the table. I could tell she was crying. It was an odd kind of crying…it's like I knew. 'Your father's had a heart attack. He's dead. I have to go to the hospital. I know you don't have a license yet, but do you think you could drive me?' As she spoke this pathetic request, she looked up into my eyes with a look of terror. 'John David, I don't know what we're gonna do. Your father had very little life insurance, just enough to bury him. I don't know what we're to do.'"

The whole way back home the two were consumed in their respective unhappiness. Dothan just stared out the passenger window while Jessica drove.

II.

The stress of work is the great reliever of personal stress. And for Dothan, there was much to be done on a professional level. His "day gig" was littered with loose ends. Mr. Langhorne, several years prior, had hired his son-in-law on as a public relations man. While this was initially an act of nepotism, Dothan would prove somewhat talented at off-the-cuff bullshit. The former singer also demonstrated the gift of persuasion. His one flaw was his lack of interest. But this lack of interest would not interfere with his success. The customers loved him.

The fact that it was Christmas Eve and Langhorne had the office functioning at full capacity was a testament to his relentless nature. Dothan, always the insolent, strolled in just before noon. He would now be met with something he was not expecting; a sort of hero's welcome. Or was it a star's?

"You're the man, JD!" A fellow salesman declared as he came out of the bathroom.

"Congrats, JD. We all knew you could do it." A young admin, who secretly had a crush on the representative-elect, concurred.

His confidence up, his new pair of boots just breaking in, Dothan emerged onto the work floor where a sea of cubicles filled with the over-worked and the under-paid sat waiting.

It was unanimous; the entire office now stood and cheered him as he made his way towards Langhorne's office.

"Hey, JD, the boss has been waiting for you," Langhorne's secretary said. She looked up at Dothan with adulation.

"Didn't mean to keep him waiting—I'm here for the grill."

"I doubt he'll roast ya. Not this time."

"Good, he doesn't want me to have him investigated by the Comptroller, now does he?"

As the door shut behind him, the big talk and bigger attitude dissolved. Langhorne was on the phone, chewing someone out. He signaled at JD to take a seat. Dothan complied and plopped down in the big black leather chair like a child at the dentist's office. Langhorne was a tall, slim man. With his crew cut and the white streaks in his hair and mustache he reminded Dothan of Peter Parker's boss from Spider Man—the consummate comic book character.

Dothan grabbed the local paper from the nearby table and flipped through it while he waited. He happened upon an article that concerned him. The headline read: "Governor calls for Select Joint Committee to address recent federal immigration reform."

In the midst of Dothan combing through the article, the comic book character hung up the phone, clearly irritated.

"Why are you wearing goddamn blue jeans?" he asked his son-in-law, without making eye contact. He began searching through his desk. "Janet!" he yelled.

"Yes, sir," the beleaguered secretary asked as she bolted into the office.

"Where are my cigarettes?"

"Sir, you told me not to tell you."

"Well, I'm ordering you to tell me now, or you're fired!"

Janet left the room and returned a moment later with a pack of Marlboro's.

"Here, Mr. Langhorne; will that be all?"

"Yes, yes. Thank you. You'll be getting a raise soon."

Janet shook her head in disapproval as she vacated the office. "She's good. Best goddamn secretary I ever had."

"Let's hope you can keep her…sir. By the way, I think the proper term is, Office Administrator…sir."

Langhorne took a slow drag from his cigarette. Exhaling, he looked long and hard at his impertinent employee. "You haven't answered my question, JD. Why are you wearing jeans?"

"It's Christmas Eve."

"Not around here it ain't. OK, enough of that shit. We've got five deals lingering. Have you talked to that son-of-a-bitch in Louisiana? What about that deal in Brazoria?"

"No, to both." Dothan always began bold.

"Why not?

"I'm sorry, sir. I've been busy with…with…everything."

"Well this is a part of everything!" Langhorne declared, crushing his smoke into the ashtray. "Figure it out."

"Yes, sir; I'll get on it immediately."

Dothan spent that night, as well as the next several days, reviewing the Louisiana and Brazoria deals respectively; neither having much in the way of private investors. All were contingent upon exacting pork, or incentives, from state governments. Both would require his ability to garner influence. Although the amount of money he and Jessica would make in the deals was sizeable, Dothan found his focus repeatedly in a fog. He constantly had to return to the documents in order to remember what it was he had just reviewed.

Christmas passed with a whimper, as it had almost all of his adult life. Once upon a time he had dreamed that success in life might revive the enchantment in life. That notion seemed as remote now as the magic he missed. Back home out on his deck, he sat at the patio table and looked out over the great gray Gulf. The sun had not shined in days.

III.

New Year's Eve was a ritual with the Dothan's. The couple had attended a masquerade function in one capacity or another since they had first begun dating. Jessica always went as a cat. For years Dothan had gone as a dead Confederate soldier, smearing white makeup on his face. There was not a hint of racism in his disguise, but the present politically incorrect nature of it had willed him to alter his costume. The last few years Dothan had gone as a vampire—very chic.

The cat and the vampire tonight were headed to a rather ritzy shindig in an exclusive neighborhood of Houston, known as River Oaks. River Oaks was the heart of "player's-ville." Although largely Republican, there were intermittently scattered among its colonial-style mansions, enclaves of liberalism. As they cruised down the freeway in Jessica's Mercedes, the couple started into their most recent past time—arguing.

"JD, you must have lipstick on your fingers or something, there's black shit all over the console!"

"Oh, I'm sorry. I hope I don't have it on my shirt. Mind if I switch on the light?"

"Goddamn, dude! I can't see the road with that on!"

"Sorry," Dothan apologized in a conciliatory fashion as he switched off the light.

"Jesus! Did you get any on your costume?"

"Yes."

"Serves you right; you really have no respect for my things. This isn't that piece of shit pickup, JD."

"It's not a piece of shit, Jessica, it's vintage—considered a classic."

"It's a piece of shit!"

Then, after a moment of agitated silence, Dothan cautiously spoke, "I went ahead and invited my new assistant, Tryphena."

"What? Why?"

"Why not? I thought she might enjoy seeing how the other side lives."

"How is she going to get there? They're not going to let her in."

"Sure they will; I had Jack contact them. It's all good."

The destination now came into view. Under an arbor of ancient oaks, the couple surrendered their car keys to the valet.

"This is nice," Dothan remarked, as he looked up at the eight giant columns.

"Beats the crap out of our beach house," Jessica added.

Once inside the vast home, structured like a maze, the two went their own directions. Dothan made his way towards the back of the house to the bar.

The corners of the vast room were littered with odd, abstract sculptures. The walls were covered in signed black and white photos of glamorous people who looked like they were starving. The bookshelves lacked books.

While standing in line at the bar, his eyes were suddenly covered by two small hands that reached around from behind him.

"You're not going to suck my blood are you?"

"Jeanie?"

"How did you know?" Jeanie said, playfully flabbergasted.

"Oh, it was the hands, I assure you," Dothan replied, facetiously. He'd turned around to greet her.

Jeanie grabbed Dothan and pulled him into her bosom, hugging him tightly. Somewhat startled, he surrendered. After a longer than appropriate embrace, Jeanie let her hostage lose. "Congrats, Count!"

"Well thank you, Marilyn."

"It's Jane Mansfield, you dummy."

"Jane Mansfield…whatever you say."

Jeanie was one of Jessica's on-again, off-again friends from college: on and off, because the two were constantly quarreling over the most insignificant of matters. While still early, she was already drunk. Dothan himself started to kill Whiskey Sours.

Tryphena would not show until much later. Unable to find her new employer, she skulked awkwardly in and out of the crowd of guests, horribly out of place. After several drinks had not calmed her nerves, she decided to take a cigarette break out on the back patio. The night, for the first time in weeks, was clear. Puffing her smoke, admiring the moon, she heard the sound of giggling, then the sound of a voice—a voice she thought she recognized. She could swear she heard Dothan as she made her way out into the garden. Two silhouetted figures, standing near the edge of the pool, came into view.

"Come on, you suck my blood, I'll suck your…"

"Jeanie, come on now. What would Jessica think?"

"Jessica's a slut!" Jeanie spewed, followed by a devilish laugh.

Tryphena emerged from behind a large live oak. She recognized the two figures that stood, partly illuminated.

"Unzip!" The buxom blond demanded, dropping to her knees.

Dothan, looking about for people, spotted Tryphena, right as Jeanie engulfed his half-limp penis.

"Tryphena?" Dothan asked, startled beyond cognizance. Tryphena could not keep from gagging. Every atom in her body cried out in revulsion. Hurrying from the patio, then through the house and to the valet, she claimed her car, leaving in disgust. *Who is this pervert I'm working for?* She questioned herself again and again on her long drive back home across the cold proverbial tracks.

chapter Four

"Please be careful with that! This was my father's Edwardian writing desk!" Dothan pleaded with the movers as they struggled to get the large mahogany piece of furniture through his office door. Today was moving day at the State Capitol in Austin. The utter lunacy of it all had the legislator out of sorts. Dothan's designated quarters were below on one of the subterranean floors deep in the bowels of the giant red granite building. After several incarnations, the present structure was finally completed in 1888. The Texas Capitol actually stands taller than the nation's capitol in Washington D.C. Freshman representatives were usually stationed as far away from its lofty dome as possible. Back and forth to the garage, where the small moving van as well as his pickup sat, was the order of the day.

Apart from the obvious anxiety over his new responsibilities, Dothan awaited with a mixture of trepidation and embarrassment the arrival of his new Chief of Staff. New Year's, just the week prior, was still in the forefront of his crowded mind. He had not spoken with Tryphena since that stained evening. He'd gone over in his head countless times, searching for an excuse. He still had little confidence in his ability to exonerate himself in her eyes.

Although January, Austin was hot enough for sweat marks to appear beneath his white shirt as he walked to and from his truck. As he made his way down the long hall towards his new office, with numerous wall ornaments under each arm, a smiling figure stopped to introduce himself.

"How are you? I'm Ron Martinez," the fellow representative said, extending his hand.

"Ron, I'm John David Dothan. Pleased to meet you, sir."

"Let me help you with those, John David."

"Please, call me JD, Ron."

"Just as I thought, you're my new neighbor. Thank God, a fellow Democrat, too," Martinez said as the two entered Dothan's office.

"We're becoming a scarce commodity around here these days, huh?"

"No doubt."

After viewing the pictures that the two comrades had just set against the freshly painted wall, Martinez commented, "Interesting choice of decoration, JD. Most guys around here have Texana they hang from their walls: Sam Houston, Jim Bowie. But you—David Bowie, Elvis Costello, U2—this is rock-n-roll, man."

"Yeah, well…that was my former profession."

"I seem to remember reading something about that. How

does a rock singer make it into the state legislature?"

"I thought it was the logical extension. Like my wife says, 'You picked the one thing sleazier than the music business.'"

"Rock-n-roll, brother."

"What kind of music do you listen to, Ron?"

"What kind of music? I don't know…whatever. I'm not into music really. I like baseball."

"You're from the valley— the border actually, aren't you?"

"Yeah, Elsa to be exact; about twenty miles from the border, near McAllen."

"Don't you have a Chief of Staff or someone? Is it just you here alone?"

"I've got one. She's coming. Be here soon."

Martinez continued assisting Dothan with the hanging of his unorthodox decor. It wasn't long before the talk turned to politics and policy.

"So tell me, JD, what's your position on the illegal issue?"

"Conflicted."

"Have you heard of the new joint committee that the governor has called?"

"Yes, as a matter of fact I have. I read about that just a few weeks ago. It's in response to that amnesty bill passed this past fall by Congress. Fueled by the subsequent deaths of those school children on the border—near your district, right?"

"Yes, that's right; it was actually in my district. But I'm not sure that the Immigration Reform Law was really the cause of the bus being bombed. I know they have not been able to prove it, but it was the cartels. Human trafficking is more profitable than drugs."

"Yeah, bad timing, I suppose."

"Well, anyway, I've got a bill ready to be filed, a State of Texas guest-worker bill. I think it addresses the issue from every angle. Bottom line is: we need to realize and utilize those who are here and want to work."

"Yeah, but Washington decides it ultimately. Even though they usually screw stuff up pretty bad—whatever it is."

"The new law doesn't go into effect for another year. I think what I have will appease them. It could use your support, JD. It's not official, but after the House and Senate file their resolutions this week, in order to get this thing going, it's a good chance I'll be the Vice Chair."

"Really! Well lucky me, stationed next door. Send it over and I'll be happy to look at it before it goes to committee. If it gets that far that is."

"It will because it has bi-partisan support. This conundrum with the Feds has opened a huge opportunity for state leadership in this area. And though I'm what some conservatives would call a 'big government' Democrat, one can't deny that recent events have hurt the Hispanic cause in this state as well as the nation. Would you be interested?"

"Interested in what, the committee?

"You're a performer. You've got a fantastic speaking voice. Maybe you could help our cause."

"I'm not sure what the cause is. Anyway, I think you over estimate my talents, Ron…and my connections. The speaker and I aren't even acquaintances. I don't really know anyone."

"We'll you know me. Think about it, JD. I mean it."

"Get me a copy of the bill."

After helping out, Martinez left. The busy day gradually died down. As the day dragged on, there was still no sign of Tryphena. Dothan sat down at his large mahogany desk, swung around in his brown leather swivel chair (which bore the state seal), and allowed himself to feel important.

A figure appeared in the doorway.

Dothan swallowed hard and wondered how he should handle this situation. *Should I stand and greet her, or stay put?* he wondered. *Should I apologize for New Year's or inform her that she was very late to her first official day on the job?* He did neither.

"Tryphena, good afternoon. Your desk will go over there," he said awkwardly, pointing towards a corner of the small office space. I ordered it several days ago. It probably won't be here 'til tomorrow. For the time being, you can put your things on top of that bookshelf over there."

"Thank you, Representative," Tryphena responded. She entered the office and gently closed the door behind her. She moved stiffly with her head hung down and placed her purse atop a tall bookshelf. She looked around for a chair.

"Oh, I'm sorry, a chair!"

As Dothan went in search of a chair, she reflected on how much this scene resembled their first meeting. But this was not their first meeting.

Dothan returned with a gray folding chair and placed it next to the bookcase. Both took their respective seats and looked awkwardly into each other's eyes. Tryphena moved her lips to speak. Dothan interrupted before more than a syllable could be uttered. Realizing after his initial utterance that he had cut in, he addressed his employee, "I'm sorry, how rude of me. Tryphena, please, you speak first."

"It's OK, sir. You can go first."

"OK. Well…look… I can't take it anymore…. About New Year's…"

"It's OK, sir. Really, sir; it's OK."

"Look, stop calling me sir. Just call me JD. OK?"

"JD?"

"Look, let me say what I'm going to say."

"Yes, sir. I mean…"

Dothan was getting agitated with the rigid formality. "Stop!"

He rose from his chair and began pacing about the room like a caged tiger. His agitation made Tryphena even more uncomfortable. Suddenly, he twirled around on the soul of his boot, stopped and took a knee in front of her.

Is he going to ask me to marry him? No way! He's already married.

"Look, I'm sorry. I'm sorry about New Year's. That was the absolute worst thing that you could have been exposed to, and… I'm sorry." He paused, waiting for an acceptance, a confirmation of his apology. When a few too many seconds passed and it did not come, he continued. "Look…"

Tryphena had had enough, and finally broke in, "Look? You keep saying that. I did look, and it was disgusting. I can't believe you are so…so…"

"So what?" Dothan asked, troubled by this reproach.

"So irresponsible, flippant, perverse, stupid…"

"Hey now, watch what you say, Tryphena."

"Watch what I say? If you want respect, sir, you should act accordingly. How do you expect to ever get anywhere doing those kinds of things? And what about your wife? I almost emailed you my resignation. I need this job, but I almost quit. Then I thought, 'no, I'll go in and tell him to his face.'"

Dothan knew he'd been defeated. Still kneeling, his head sank low.

Tryphena, still seated, gazed down at the back of his head—studying the thick black locks. *He seems so sad*, she mused. Tryphena wanted badly to run her fingers through his hair. Not in a wanton way, but a maternal one.

There was a knock at the door.

"Who can that be?" Dothan asked bolting up from the floor.

"JD. Hey, sorry to bother you, but here's the latest draft of that bill I was telling you about earlier."

Dothan took the heft of unbound paper as Martinez realized the presence of another: a very attractive third party. "Oh, I'm sorry miss, my name is Ron Martinez, Representative Ron Martinez."

"Pleased to meet you, Representative Martinez." she said, lifting her frame proudly from her chair, "I'm Tryphena Taylor, Representative Dothan's new Chief of Staff." She shook Martinez's hand and gazed subtly over at Dothan; a self-assured smirk accompanied her dark eyes.

Dothan stood there, startled. He regained his composure, "Yes Ron, Tryphena is my new assistant…very sharp."

"Is that right? Lucky you. Have you ever worked up at the Capitol before, Ms. Taylor?

"No, no I haven't. Representative Dothan was kind enough to hire a rookie."

"Well JD," Martinez said, "I must be going; I have a meeting with the speaker. Let's keep our fingers crossed."

The employee and the employer now stood awkwardly alone together.

The matter concerning that one ludicrous New Year Eve… was settled.

~

The next few days were lonely ones for Tryphena. Dothan, though in the building, was rarely present. He was on the floor, at caucus meetings or attending functions, as well as the inauguration ceremony; all this took the bulk of his time.

Tryphena was charged with the task of organizing the chaos of the representative's office. Similar to the district office in Matagorda, there were many boxes of books, even more here than there. Thankfully, the small office was wall-to-wall bookshelves.

She knew that arranging the vast array of volumes would take time and she delved into the task with abandon. Most of the inventory consisted of reference books dealing with legislative history, bills, etc. A healthy number of volumes existed on history of all sorts. Poetry eclipsed the other subjects. The poets were varied and Tryphena did not recognize many of the authors. She was disappointed there was not one volume of either Langston Hughes or Dereck Walcott while books by and about the poet Shelley abounded. She lifted an aged, hardback of poems by the great Romantic and a photograph fell from between the pages and landed on the floor.

"What's this?" she wondered out loud.

She picked up the small, wallet-sized picture and gazed at the subject. It was of a very young woman of olive complexion and chestnut hair. The cheekbones were high, the nose slim, the jaw defined. Her dress, visible from the bosom, was an elegant red. She turned the photo over and read the faded writing: *"To John David, from the Rose of your memory, Love Rachael."*

"The Rose of your memory," she repeated, "I like that." *Who was she?* she wondered.

She placed the photo back in-between the yellowed pages.

JD is quite the lure, what with his contradictions and mysteries, quite the lure, indeed.

II.

"JD, what in the hell is this tome I have sitting on my desk?" the voice on the other end of the phone asked angrily.

"Well sir, it's a house bill I wanted you to take a look at. It's been authored by a fellow rep. and it's going to go before that new joint committee the governor has called for.

"It's a goddamn State Amnesty bill, JD. Hasn't the federal government already fucked this up enough?" The voice was that of Dothan's employer and father-in-law.

"It's a guest-worker bill, sir. Though it's not perfect…"

"Same damn difference!" Langhorne interrupted.

There was a protracted silence on the line. After taking a deep breath, Langhorne tried to instill reason into his newly elected plant. "JD, we're in the construction business. That means we use illegals, right?"

The question was rhetorical and not meant to be answered.

"Look, I don't give a damn about some new constituency for the Democratic Party. I care about money. And if I have to document workers, that means I have to deal with payroll taxes, workers comp, and all kinds of bureaucratic bullshit. The way I see it, the more under the radar the better. We don't need some crusade to enfranchise the goddamn Mexicans! I don't give a shit if they're apart of the American Dream or not. Truth-be-told, nobody in Austin or Washington does either. They just see votes. It's a damn lie. Think about it this way, Mr. Idealist, once the illegals are as expensive as the natives, then what?"

Dothan, as usual, sat silent, not knowing how to respond. At his core, he felt his father-in-law to be a fiend. But his intellect knew better. His intellect told him that Langhorne was right. It was all a lie.

"We're just now forming a committee. It won't go anywhere, sir."

"It better not!"

JD hung up the phone. His mind wandered back to a thought that often plagued him—the reality that he had been born on the backend of possibility. The dreamers had come and gone and the azure kingdom they had labored with their lives to construct, torn to shreds. Unable to bear the weight of it, he defaulted back into his innate utopianism.

~

At week's end, Dothan drove home. He had intended to stay in Austin that weekend and did not inform his wife of his return. As he approached his home, with the night air as fresh as showered skin, Dothan noticed the silhouette of a vehicle in his driveway. The automobile did not resemble any he owned or recognized. He killed the headlights and the engine of the Ford and stealthily coasted into the drive. He opened a beer from his six-pack and sat in the darkness, his heart beating rapidly.

A figure moved past the bedroom window. His heart beat faster. He swilled down the dregs of his drink and got out of his truck, leaving the door wide open. He paced uncertain to the front door of his home. He felt like a stranger, or worse, an intruder.

There was no one present as he gently closed the squeaking door. Then, from the shadows of the hallway, a figure appeared. Dothan switched on the light and felt his adrenaline surge. "Who the fuck are you?" he shouted at the man standing in his den.

"Oh, oh…I'm a massage therapist! I am here consulting your wife!"

"Consulting her on how to purr like a kitten I bet."

"That's ridiculous JD!" Jessica retorted from the hall. "Rico is my new masseuse." She emerged from the shadow, wearing only a long navy blue robe.

"Since when do you have a masseuse?"

"Since my back started hurting again and your state insurance kicked-in. It covers everything." Jessica stood, hands on her hips, in a self-righteous pose. Dothan stood perplexed and distraught.

"I was just going out to my car to get some oils, Mr. Dothan. I'm leaving them here with your wife. Then I go."

Rico's Euro-trash accent irritated Dothan. As the man vacated and then reentered, leaving the articles behind, Jessica stared with indignation at her ridiculous husband. "I'm taking a shower," she said, plainly.

Dothan had not moved. He stared across the den, into the next room at the dated design on the kitchen wallpaper, he pondered an ancient question: *The men women cheat on their husbands with, why?* He knew that women cheated, and understood why at some level, it was who they cheated with that seemed… bizarre. And while he understood why Jessica would want someone different, *would she really go for a complete opposite?* Where Dothan was tall, Rico was short. Dothan's hair, a thick mane of jet-black, Rico's a thinning (obviously peroxide-dyed) blond. Dothan was thin. Rico was short and tubby. "Uggh," he gagged.

He walked into the kitchen and grabbed a beer from the refrigerator. He couldn't get Rico out of his head. The man was definitely no porn star. *Or maybe he was? Maybe he has the equipment?* The whole thing made Dothan cringe.

He heard the faint hum of running water and his heart's rebellion subsided. The conquering mind, intervening, rationalized: *Rico is an employee, nothing more…or is it more?* Back and forth he went.

When Jessica finished her bath, she dressed and went out without saying a word. From his office, lit only by a solitary lamp, he heard the door shut then the revving of the engine. He followed the drone until it was out of earshot, then he resumed the task at hand—an endeavor he had not undertaken in sometime—writing verse. An hour and six beers later, he had completed his meditation—a sonnet.

The Cheating Wife

What was it that brought her to this point?
The brutish things he said but never heard?
Her learning that the beast was not a prince;
And yet recalling that the beast was the lure?

Was it liberating? Certainly not,
Her guilt rallied around her like a mob.
And thus within this irony her true pain lay;
Having become the Diana that shed her lace.

But the flippant sheets she thought she sought
Were fetid at best, like trash to be took out.
A child extinguished in the womb:
Her enterprise foiled by her femininity.

What was it that brought her to this point?
To find that feral spark in her refuge soft?

He read it out loud and then reread it to himself over and over again. He concluded that it had no merit and tossed it in the wastebasket.

∾

The Texas House of Representatives officially convened that Thursday. Representative John David Dothan was fashionably late, very unfashionable for a freshman member of the minority party. The learning curve was considerable, but not cumbersome.

The clerk read Representative Martinez's bill on the floor of the House. The Speaker sent it to the Select Joint Committee on Immigration Reform; a committee that Martinez had subsequently been appointed to as Vice Chairman.

Representative John David Dothan was appointed as well, the only freshman to have this distinction.

Across the gaping mouth of the rotunda the Senate swarmed in their respective chamber.

chapter Five

The phone rang endlessly and Tryphena felt more like a receptionist than a chief of staff. Lobbyists continuously arrived unannounced and monopolized her time. She could not get anything done. A file containing resumes of potential receptionist candidates sat largely ignored. Dothan had entered the Capitol essentially unprepared with regards to staff. All the other offices on their hallway had interns, legislative advisors, and the like. Dothan had only Tryphena.

The day was drawing to a close. She did what she could in between calls to make her representative's new office look less like a dungeon. When five o'clock struck, though willing to remain in order to review resumes, she decided to ignore the phone. A single number that kept appearing on the caller I.D. constantly interrupted her concentration. No name was listed.

She finally answered, "Hello, Representative Dothan's office. May I help you?"

"Who is this?" A husky feminine voice blurted from the other end.

"This is Representative Dothan's Chief of Staff, Tryphena Taylor, ma'am."

"Don't go thinking you're all that, Sugar. JD's always been good at making the help feel more important than they are. And not out of benevolence, I assure you. He always gets something out of it."

The attitude of this woman was hard to take. But Tryphena maintained her composure. "Um, may I ask who this is?" She intuitively knew the answer before the woman in question answered.

"Mrs. Dothan. And where's my husband?"

"Representative Dothan is in a meeting, Ms. Dothan."

"He'll always just be JD to me. And will ultimately be just that to you too, I'll bet." There was a pause, Mrs. Dothan continued, "Just tell him to call me. And not too late, I have a backache. I'll be going to bed soon."

After hanging up, Tryphena could not contain her spleen. "What a bitch!" The words had just left her lips when she realized the door to the office was wide open. She quickly rose from her desk to close it. She stood in the doorway and peered down both sides of the long empty hallway. Thankfully, she was alone.

She returned to her chair and began to ponder the odd conversation of just a few moments ago. *What was that all about? It's like she had something to prove. Weird.* Still, based on recent events, she could not discard entirely the reproaches of Mrs. John David Dothan...*but what a bitch.*

Sometime around 9:00p.m., she finally finished organizing what she needed so she could hit the ground running in the morning. She left a note for her employer, informing him that his wife had called. She stood and grabbed her things to go, but as she was locking up the office, a loud deep voice echoed from somewhere. She saw coming down the corridor, two dark suited figures—one dwarfing the other. It was Representatives' Dothan and Martinez, returning from their committee meeting.

Well Ms. Taylor, still working are you?" Martinez asked as they approached. "You got lucky here JD, lucky indeed. I will tell you Ms. Taylor, if your employer doesn't fawn over you and your performance each and every day, let me know." He turned to Dothan and prodded him in jest, "What are you paying her, JD? I'll double it."

Tryphena liked Martinez because, so far, he had always maintained a Latin chivalry towards her. "I will let you know Representative Martinez, I assure you," she said.

"Call me, Ron."

After a few more moments of triviality, tempered with bits of business, Martinez excused himself. Tryphena and Dothan stood awkwardly alone for a moment outside his office.

"So, I guess you're heading home?" he asked, acknowledging the obvious.

"Yes, I'm headed home." Their relationship had taken on a strange dichotomy. Their interaction was less like employer/employee, more like two co-workers who shared a forbidden secret. It was too close, and as such, was ironically uncomfortable.

As Tryphena walked down the corridor, she paused, turned around, and called to him, "Your wife called."

"My wife?"

"Yeah, I left you a sticky note on your computer."

"My wife…hmm. Thank you."

"Oh, and just to let you know, I won't be available on Friday. I have to go back to Houston so I can take my dad to the hospital for some tests he has scheduled."

This was short notice, but given the circumstances, Dothan refrained from comment other than, "I'll make do. Goodnight Tryphena."

Once at his computer, he stared perplexed at the sticky note. *What could she want?* He really didn't want to make the call. The day's events had been laborious enough. Now he was expected to call his wife. *I need a drink.* Dothan just wanted to get out of there. So he did.

He stopped by a convenience store on the way back to his apartment and picked up some adult refreshment. He had just signed the lease this past weekend to his new digs just off of Congress Avenue, not far from the Capitol. In fact, he could just make out the dome from the small porch of his second story patio when the lights cut through the drought stricken branches.

He collapsed onto his sofa and popped open a lukewarm beer. Suddenly, it dawned on him that he had not called Jessica back. He checked his cell phone and saw she had called that number as well. He slammed down the brew and hit her contact name on his device.

"What?" Jessica sounded as if she had been asleep.

"Jessica?"

"JD, what time is it?"

"I don't know, sometime after nine. If you're sleeping I can call back in the morning."

"Didn't that…what's her name… tell you not to call too late. My back hurts!"

"Goddamn it Jessica, it's only nine o'clock. And her name's Tryphena!"

"Oh, that just rolls off your tongue, doesn't it, JD?"

"What are you talking about?"

"What am I talking about? What are you talking about?"

"What, wait…why did you call?"

"I called to let you know that I talked to Daddy today. He wants us to come up to Austin. Check on his investment."

"Investment? You know I hate it when you call me that, Jessica!"

"I know. Isn't it funny?"

He didn't laugh and just asked, "When?"

"In the next couple of weeks, I'm sure."

"You can come up, but I can't guarantee that I'll be available. I have a job to do—we're in session."

"We'll see. So how old is she, JD?"

"Who? How old is who?"

"Try…whatever-her-name-is."

"Tryphena. She's twenty-four."

"Is that right? She sounds black. Is she?"

"Yes."

"You and Slick Willy: Two peas in a pod."

"I'm going to let you go now."

"Ok, but in a couple of weeks."

"We'll see. Goodbye."

As soon as the call disconnected, he threw his cell phone at the wall. It ricocheted off of numerous pieces of furniture and came to a rest beside his boot.

"Goddamn it," he complained when he discovered that the screen had been irreparably compromised, "I'll have to get another phone…and my contacts!" he lamented.

He brooded as he polished off the six-pack "I might as well end the day," he resolved. What a day it had been! It was only Monday, and he was ready for the weekend.

Sleep evaded him. As he tossed and turned, his mind kept going over and over the meeting he and Martinez had been in that afternoon. *What has Ron gotten me into?* he thought. It had been announced earlier that day on the floor of the House that Dothan had been appointed to the "Select Joint Committee on Immigration Reform." With no time to prepare, he cut his teeth with the group. This committee was stacked with twice as many Republicans than Democrats, with apparently more "Elephants" on the way.

Nothing had been accomplished thus far because neither side had, as of yet, produced a leader. It seemed to Dothan a load of nonsense. The Chairman, Senator Jackson, was not present, leaving Ron to run the show. During every break, Martinez pressured Dothan to use his oratorical skills. Dothan, a novice, was not yet convinced of his "skills." And besides, he had no idea what to say.

Thought beget thought, and soon he was worried about Langhorne. *What will his reaction be once he discovers I'm on this committee?* Dothan fretted.

~

Morning found him grappling with a fit of diarrhea, but a bottle of Pepto would assuage it. With a slight hangover he confronted a new day.

"I tried calling you last night, but it went straight to voice-mail." Ron informed him as they strode quickly towards the House floor.

"Yeah, I dropped it in the toilet by accident. I'm gonna have to get another one. Remember to write your contact info down for me, would you?"

II.

Friday took forever to finally raise its triumphant fist. What a week it had been. Dothan was not by nature confrontational, but he was getting an education in conflict. Sitting in Martinez's office, the two went over the first week of proposals: rejections and emotions.

"JD, I wish you'd be more assertive when discussing the plan."

"I'm a freshman, Ron. Frankly, getting in people's faces makes me uncomfortable."

"You need to," Martinez said.

"Apparently."

"Look, nobody speaks as well as you. I mean shit, you're the only guy I know who can drop those big words without looking like a pretentious ass."

"Yeah, I believe in the plan, I just wish we could get more of these damn Republicans to acquiesce."

"That's what I mean, 'acquiesce!'"

"Right," Dothan replied with an embarrassed chuckle.

"There are a couple of senators who will be coming in next week. I guess we'll see how things go."

"Do you know who they are?"

"Well, Jackson is Chairman, of course. He's been out—down in the Valley on Home Land Security stuff; and Rachael Logan, his protégé."

"Never met them."

"That's right, you missed the Legislative Mixer."

"Yeah, I had an emergency with one of my father-in-law's clients. It was BS. What do you know about Jackson and Logan?"

"Well, Jackson, Reed Jackson, he's an old bastard; arrogant; institutional."

"I think he was in the tank for my former opponent. That is until the dirt was delivered. And Logan?"

"A woman in her late thirties early forties. Pretty; staunch Pro-Life advocate."

"Lord help us!"

"Oh JD, you're such a heathen," Martinez retorted in jest. "It's all that rock-n-roll, man!"

~

Luckily, the rest of the day didn't have much on the agenda. That morning, the committee had convened for the weekend; the members met only briefly to distribute a vast amount of paperwork; paperwork that Dothan largely disregarded.

Dothan was grateful for the lax schedule because Tryphena was absent, dealing with her father. Dothan returned to his lonely office and tried combing through some of the morning's amendments. From a cursory review of the committee paperwork, a clause sent out from Senator Logan's office caught his eye.

"You're kidding me!" he shouted out in surprise.

Dothan was elated; his weekend made. He had entered into this committee both green and utterly skeptical. The past week had only confirmed his apprehension. But now, there was a proposal—from a Republican, which struck him as not only workable—but ingenious. This was somebody he wanted to meet. Browsing over the committee information he looked for Logan's office number. It was upstairs.

He jumped up from his desk, grabbed his coat and sprinted out of the office, leaving the door wide open. It was late and there was little wait for an elevator. The hallway upstairs was dauntingly long. Nevertheless, Dothan scanned the doors trying to find the correct name and number. Upon locating the correct office, he discovered that it was locked and no light illuminated through the tempered glass. His elation leveling, he journeyed back downstairs, nonetheless inspired.

He searched through his library—the library that Tryphena had organized, looking for the Texas Legislative Handbook. He desperately wished to put a face on this particular state senator. Just as he found the right publication, he heard a knock on his door. He assumed it was Martinez and went to welcome him in. The hall light was turned off, making it difficult to determine who the figure was standing on the other side of the glass. A harder knock followed, suddenly filling Dothan with a sense of dread. He opened the door and discovered his wife and father-in-law.

"Damn JD, what the hell was keeping you?" Langhorne belted out, clearly irritated.

"Oh just working on some things in my office. Sorry, sir. What brings the two of you here this late…and unannounced? Dothan asked, looking accusingly at Jessica.

"Unannounced, hell, I'm never unannounced, JD!" Langhorne retorted, turning around to face the two after placing his coat on the coat rack.

"Why don't ya'll come back into my office, take a seat?"

"Jesus JD, this place looks like a teenager lives here," Langhorne observed with his customary disrespect.

Langhorne and his daughter sat fidgeting in their dark red leather chairs as they stared over the large mahogany desk at Representative John David Dothan.

"This place looks like the bedroom of a Goddamn teenager!" Langhorne declared again.

Dothan was only partly present. One third of his attention was fixated on the book of legislators that lay in front of him on his desk; one third swam in the euphoric realization that it was his office that the two guests sat in and not the other way around. The last, unfortunately, was spent listening to his father-in-law rant.

"It's come to my attention that the project in Brazoria might run into problems because of some Environmental Assessment Study or some shit."

"Right, they do this on almost every project we've done in the last few years," Dothan replied.

"One problem here, however, apparently there is some issue with aquatic something-or-other. Hell, I don't know! I need you to figure this out for me, JD!"

At this point, Jessica decided to chime in, "No one wants to hurt the environment JD, as our hefty checks to the Sierra Club will attest, but Daddy needs a way around some unneeded, expensive study."

"Right!" Langhorne affirmed.

"This is a federal issue, sir."

The two guests now engaged in a heated discussion between themselves, as if Dothan were not there. Slyly moving the handbook into his sight, he resumed the search for one, Rachael Logan. As he searched for the page number listed in the contents, he suddenly realized that the discussion had stopped.

"Are you going to listen to Daddy or read that book?" Jessica asked haughtily.

"Sorry."

"There's a fella I know in Washington. I've got his information here. I need to make a phone call," Langhorne said.

"Sure, sir, by all means," Dothan said, pushing the apparatus towards Langhorne. "Just dial the number, no problem."

"Long distance OK?"

"You're in the State Capitol, of course."

Jessica resumed her fidgeting while Langhorne began his conversation with Washington. Dothan, freed up at last, gazed at his book again, thumbing his way towards the desired page. The page found, his eyes combed the column of senators' photographs.

Life is lived at its most intense while experiencing the unexpected: That dash or surge of electricity that fills a person with a sense of both adrenaline and dread simultaneously. Dothan tore a sticky note from its pad, folded it in half, and marked this specific page. He was now in a world far removed from the one that contained his wife and ranting father-in-law.

Are you OK JD?" Jessica asked, noticing that his breathing was abnormal.

Langhorne, trying to carry on his important conversation, waved at his daughter to shut up.

Dothan smiled at his wife unconvincingly.

Once finished with his long distance talk, Langhorne placed the phone down with an air of contentment. "That fella's alright. I might be able to do business with that man. He's a lobbyist in D.C. I got the number from the Texas Builders' Association. Proven to be more helpful than you so far JD."

The business for that evening was complete. Langhorne insisted that he take his daughter and Dothan to dinner. Dothan sat polite but distracted.

~

When Tryphena opened the office up that Monday morning she found a mess. Dothan was no organizer. Files and folders sat on chairs and on the floor, everywhere but in their place. On Dothan's desk she discovered the procured handbook, a small piece of yellow paper protruding from its pages. Opening to the designated page, she was hit profoundly by the unexpected.

chapter six

Dothan stood outside the committee room trying to pat the sweat from his neck, face and forehead. *Am I having an anxiety attack?* he wondered. Most of the committee was already in the room and seated. He was late as usual.

Martinez suddenly emerged from behind the closed doors and saw his restless colleague in the hall. "JD, you alright there man?" he inquired.

"Yeah, I'm fine…I think I ate something bad. I don't feel very good, Ron."

"Well go back to your office, or to the men's room, whichever one you think you need. Sit this one out. I really think you should, brother."

"You sure that's alright? I mean…this is the first meeting with the chairman and what not."

"Man, you got lots to learn my friend. You've got plenty of time. By the way, what and where did you eat?"

"Don't worry, it wasn't from the cafeteria, you bastard."

"Alright, buddy." Martinez chuckled and patted Dothan on the shoulder. "You go do what you need to do. I'll cover for ya', JD."

Once back at his office, Dothan immediately felt relieved. Then regret settled in. The uneasiness returned—he felt like a coward. He reached into one of his file cabinets and removed a bottle of Pepto-Bismol.

Tryphena, returning from the restroom, entered the office. "Representative Dothan, aren't you supposed to be in a meeting?

"What?" he asked, startled; he turned around to face her.

"Are you OK?" she asked, noticing the pink bottle in his hand.

"Yes," Dothan answered after gulping the bottle's entire contents.

"Oh my God, did you read the label? That's like ten times too big of a dose!"

"What? I don't care. I'm late. I've got to go!"

"Well, wipe that pink rim from around your mouth before you go in to the meeting!"

Dothan brushed past her, almost rudely, and charged down the hallway towards the meeting he was missing. Tryphena was left feeling troubled about him as usual. Her instincts told her the true reason for the incident that had just played out.

The doors loomed before him. Clutching his briefcase tightly, Dothan entered the meeting. Ron Martinez was in the middle of addressing the committee.

"Well, speak of the devil. There he is. I was just telling our group here that you were ill. I guess you're trying to make a liar out of me, huh, JD?"

The entire room feigned laughter.

Dothan swallowed hard and spoke, "Yes, I'm sorry everyone. Something I ate for lunch did not agree with me; nothing a little Pepto can't resolve, though. I'm ready for battle." Dothan grabbed a seat at the first available chair.

The table was a large mahogany oval, where nine senators and representatives sat. The room itself omitted a brown aura. It was barely large enough to accommodate the table. Uncomfortable, Dothan had not yet surveyed the room.

Martinez took control. "Chairman Reed and Senator Logan, I would like to introduce you to Representative John David Dothan."

Two voices sounded their hellos in succession. One was across the table, to the right. The other was clearly female, but he could not see her as she was on his side of the table, to the left. Her back had been to the entry door.

Dothan knew he needed to stand and greet the two. Rising, he nodded at Reed Jackson who nodded back with an air of rigid plasticity. He turned left and gazed down on a presence out of the past. Suddenly, Dothan was struck with an immense confusion: *Should I acknowledge her as a past relation or simply say hello and sit down,* he wondered. Dothan chose the latter.

He looked across at Martinez and noticed that Ron was signaling something, pointing to his mouth. Remembering what Tryphena had called out as he was leaving his office, he rubbed the pink powder from his lips. Embarrassed and uncomfortable, he sat listening as the committee discussed the infant legislation. He wished he had another bottle of Pepto. He said nothing.

Vice Chair Ron Martinez, who served as de facto chair on the committee, now rose to make a few remarks. "Folks, taking what we had previously worked on, and enhancing it considerably, is one of our newest members to The Select Joint Committee on Immigration Reform—Mrs. Rachael Logan. Rachael, the floor's all yours."

Dothan felt an intense tingle shooting up his spine. His breathing became labored…and what of his heart? It was suddenly immersed in that chaos which is exclusive to its precincts. From the corner of his eye he witnessed a tan figure rise from the table. From the table the figure passed him from behind, emerging before the small assembly.

It's her, he thought, awed.

John David Dothan understood not a word Rachael Logan said in her twenty-minute presentation; he merely sat, his eyes fixed on this creature before him; the sound of her voice a lilting that mesmerized him.

After she finished, questions were solicited. Several of the members inquired as to this and that. Dothan sat silent. Rachael Logan, through the duration of her presentation, never once looked Dothan in the eye.

Martienez spoke a few words in closing and then passed around the committee's homework, adjourning the meeting. Rachael was ensnared immediately with a swarm of bodies seeking to congratulate her, in order to increase favor.

Dothan remained seated; pretending to review the printed material passed out by Martinez.

Rachael gradually guided her milieu of sycophants to her

original position at the table. Shaking a few remaining hands, stuffing the paperwork in her briefcase, she exited politely but swiftly.

～

That night, Dothan stood on the balcony of his apartment and chain-smoked.

Come morning, the bewildered representative's chest hurt when he inhaled. More alarmingly, his pulse felt awkward. Dothan suffered from hypertension, as did his father before him. He was diagnosed in his early thirties. For the past decade he had been on medication. A regimen he was less than responsible at.

"Shit!" he exclaimed after checking his blood pressure. He tossed the cuff on the couch and began rummaging through old prescription bottles, looking for a stray blood pressure pill—he was unsuccessful. His exacerbating worry resolved itself when he began to recall yesterday's meeting. Recalling it only drew out more memories. Soon the man was consumed in instance after instance of nostalgia and he forgot about the pills.

However, time was not a commodity that was his to squander.

～

When Dothan arrived at the Capitol midmorning, Tryphena barraged him with work.

"I can't focus on any of this, right now!" he bellowed.

She noticed Representative Dothan's irritation and backed off. "These things can wait, but I suggest you at least take this report home and study it before your next meeting."

"Can't you just read it and brief me?"

"I have read it, I can brief you. But I think you need to read it yourself. It says some things that you need a firsthand knowledge of. That's my advice."

"Very well, just put it in my briefcase," he said, rising from his desk.

"Where are you going, sir?"

"I'll be back later, Tryphena. Hold down the fort."

"The fort, sir? she asked sarcastically.

"The office for Christ's sakes!"

"Yes, sir."

Dothan quickly strode to the elevator. He was a man on a mission. Somewhere, buried deep within him was the man that the world, and disappointment, had almost extinguished. Like a mythical stag, that man now appeared through the thicket. Breathing heavily and fighting back a rebellious gut, he paced the elevator floor, waiting for the doors to open. Upon opening, he was jettison.

"Yes, I would like to speak with Senator Logan, please."

"Do you have an appointment, Mr...?" The receptionist asked, startled by his intensity.

"Representative Dothan. No, I don't have an appointment."

"Well sir, if you would like to make an appointment, I'm sure Senator Logan will be happy to meet with you."

"Could you just tell her that I'm here, please?" Dothan more demanded than asked.

"It's OK Caitlin. I can see Mr. Dothan now," a plaintive voice stated plainly from behind him.

Dothan turned and his eyes met Rachael's for the first time in more than twenty years.

"Hello, John David."

"I haven't been called that in long time."

The receptionist looked confused.

"Caitlin, would you please go down to the library and look into the drunk driving stats of undocumented workers? I'd like only the last five years, please."

"Yes, ma'am." Caitlin methodically gathered her things.

Dothan stood stiff; Rachael was at ease.

Once the receptionist was gone the two just stared at each other for a moment. Dothan felt his stag slipping back into obscurity.

Rachael broke the standoff. "Congratulations on your victory. It's my understanding that your candidacy was a long a shot. Good job, John David."

Dothan detected a slight patronizing tone in her delivery. He let it go. "Thank you. Yes, it was a trial. More than I expected in fact—brutal really," he replied, leaning against the wall, crossing his legs, and his arms.

"That's campaigning for you; never a dull moment. How are you?"

"I'm fine. I guess I'm just a little confused." The stag was back.

"Confused over what?"

"Confused over why you've been ignoring me."

"Funny, I thought you were ignoring me."

"Ignoring you? I didn't even know you were in the Senate. Rachael Logan?"

"Yes, I got married. It happens you know. I'm Mrs. Donald Logan."

The air was not thinning, but getting thicker.

Rachael continued, "Look, I'm sorry John David. I didn't know how to act. It was very confusing for me as well. You know that Reed Jackson and I have been colleagues since I first entered the legislature almost ten years ago?"

"You and Reed Jackson are friends? Lord. Well, okay; so what?"

"'So what?' So what, is that I'm sorry…sorry for not coming to see you the first day of the session; telling you hello and wishing you the best. I knew you were here, but I…I'm sorry John David." Rachael's tone had transformed. She was convincing.

He peeled his form from the wall and paced the room with his hands in his pockets, staring at the floor.

Rachael continued, "We have our work cut out for us. This bill has some potential. Although the Feds will most likely sue if we do anything at all."

"Then it's all for show?" Dothan sharply retorted, looking up at her.

"I didn't say that. I simply meant that it's complicated."

"I really liked your offerings. They were equanimous. I think it has potential, as well."

"Still using big words nobody understands, I see," Rachael replied, smiling adoringly. Dothan's boyish smirk did strange things to the woman.

"Yeah, maybe."

Gazing casually around the front office, Dothan noticed numerous family portraits. Several included two children: a boy and girl. "Are those *your* children?" he asked, pointing to the pictures.

"Yes, they are: Matthew and Kathryn."

Dothan looked at her with an air of puzzlement, clenching his eyebrows and cocking his head.

"They're both adopted," she commented.

"Oh, that's fantastic. Congratulations on your family, Rachael."

"Yes, they're wonderful. Matthew's ten and Kathryn's six. They're good too. I hear horror stories about other peoples' children. I guess I'm blessed in that regard. Do you have any children of your own, John David?"

"No, I don't. I am married, however. To Jessica Langhorne, daughter of Langhorne Construction."

"Yes, I knew that."

"I guess you probably would, being friends with Reed Jackson."

Disregarding this subtle, but obvious jab, Rachael approached Dothan and placed her hands on the shoulders of his black, well-tailored suit. "I'm looking forward to working with you, John David, both in our committee and in general. I'm so glad you're here, and I want you as a co-sponsor if this bill takes flight. And I'm so very proud of you. You've come a long way from your days as a singer."

The shimmer in her eyes belied the patronizing nature of such a statement. But Dothan had grown used to it, particularly from Republicans.

The two parted. Both with a feeling the exact opposite from the outset of their meeting: Dothan strode the hall with an air of contentment, Rachael, remaining in her office, was fraught with a sense of unease.

But the spell of peace would prove short-lived. Returning to his office, Dothan was reminded of reality's default ugliness.

"Representative Dothan." Pam, his recently hired receptionist, addressed him, meekly.

"Yes Pam, what is it?"

"Well sir, Ms. Taylor had to leave suddenly while you were out. Her father was found out by the vending machine of her apartment. He had fallen out of his wheelchair and was unconscious."

"My God! Do you know what hospital he's at?"

"No sir, she didn't say."

Dothan hastily retired back into his office. So much was swimming around in his mind that he closed the door behind him—something he rarely did. He turned on his computer and stared out into space, waiting for it to boot. His thoughts were not of the crisis at hand, however, but far from it. They were of how lovely Rachael looked, and how well preserved. She looked ten years younger at least, and so much better than his wife, Jessica.

Dressed as she had been these past two occasions in her fitted skirts, she had retained that elegance that first attracted the young singer to her so long ago. He pulled out his book of Shelley and turned to the picture that marked "Prometheus Unbound." He removed the wallet-sized photograph and held it up to the light, believing that it had been tucked away undisturbed for years. He was unaware that Tryphena had recently discovered it quite by accident. Gazing longingly at the picture, he flipped it over and read the writing: *The Rose of your Memory.*

How prophetic he was to grant her that title. He was sinking now, the undertow of his memory pulling him away from the present. The phone rang. Pam answered.

"Representative Dothan!" she cried, knocking on his door.

"What is it, Pam?" he pleaded. His mind was still fuzzy.

"Ms. Taylor is on the phone, sir!"

Bursting with sudden alertness, he reached for the phone; Dothan felt a tremendous foreboding. "Yes, Tryphena, what's going on?"

"Sir," she was sobbing.

"Tryphena, try to calm down. What is it?"

"They think my father had a massive stroke. They're rushing him into a CAT scan. Nobody knows how long he lay by that vending machine. I'm so scared."

"Well stay down there; don't worry about anything up here. We'll make it fine. Do what you have to do. You have my cell phone. I want you to call me if you need anything. And let me know the status of your dad when you get to Houston. Hang in there, Tryphena!"

Tryphena was nearly hysterical when the two hung up.

Dothan and Pam were left just staring worriedly at each other.

"It looks like we might be on our own for a while, Pam."

"Yes, sir."

~

This over-eventful day finally came to a conclusion. With Pam gone, Dothan again retired to the privacy of his office, his mind not on Rachael, but Tryphena. For a time, staring into oblivion, he dwelled on the oddity of human relationships, the fragility of it all. Even Tryphena, who was as solid as a rock, was at her core completely vulnerable.

Dothan needed a beer.

~

Once home, having changed his clothes, he was again sitting on his balcony smoking a cigarette and swigging a beer. For a change, he thought of nothing.

~

The two legislators did not see each other for the rest of the week. Both headed home to their respective districts: Dothan to the Gulf

Coast, Rachael to DFW. Their opposite drives were spent dwelling on one another. Time is indeed relative. Ten years ago, ten years prior, seemed an eternity. Now, twenty-plus years on, the past seemed clearer and closer than ever.

chapter Seven

Before Dothan hit the open road, he found himself taking a detour; almost without thinking. This was Austin after all. And Austin held a special place in the pantheon of his memories. Twenty years ago the University Tower, like the Capitol dome itself, defined the Austin landscape, but no longer. The slim, phallic relic now acted as a homing beacon.

He exited onto Guadalupe, aka "The Drag," and faced another bitter disappointment. The once unique strip of coffee shops and bookstores was now a morass of generic corporate logos, like those seen in any city in America. This disgusted Dothan. But the disgust was overtaken by fascination at how brazenly he was trespassing, despite the generic signs and foreign structures, within the pillars of his Pantheon.

To his right, there appeared something that he had not thought of for two-plus decades: a simple convenience store. Although the name had most likely changed, (he did not remember it), the structure and parking lot remained intact. Indeed, the garbage dumpster itself conjured familiarity. He passed by and then decided to turn around. He pulled into the compact parking lot, got out of his car, entered the establishment and headed for the beer cooler. He experienced a vague feeling, like one sensing himself through a familiar room in pitch-blackness. Dothan exited with his beverage, stopped and surveyed the concrete as cars went blowing by.

It was nearing dark. While not quite the scene he recalled from his youth, with remnants of the day still lingering, it was close enough. Suddenly, he craved a cigarette.

～

Who was Rachael Logan? To start with she wasn't always Rachael Logan. Born Rachael Downs, she first caught Dothan's eye his senior year in high school, here in Austin. She most likely would have captured the budding rock singer's attention much sooner, but having relocated his last year of high school to a fresh institution, this was circumstance.

It was nothing scandalous, involving delinquency or the like, that precipitated this relocation, but simply to keep his band intact. Dothan's band mates had all been a year older; and all were now freshman at the distinguished university. Leaving the world of security during one's senior year took guts, and an unflinching belief in one's ordained destiny. Dothan possessed both to a fault. He lived on the floor fellow band member's apartment; life was rough and simple, but free. Unbound at last from his doting mother, who he had reluctantly persuaded to allow this unorthodox transition and arrangement, the young man found himself enthralled with the prospect of adventure.

The year passed largely without incident. Groupies and high school girls revolved around them, periodically. They were not the focus, however. Art was all. In fact, Dothan was so smitten with his own effortless ability to feed his need to create, that he could qualify as a narcissist. Of course, all this was lost on the eighteen-year-old. Ensconced in the stoic indestructibility that was once young American manhood, the boy marched on fearlessly. Love was a dream, never yet realized.

It was a typical spring night in Austin, mid-April to be exact. While it was a little warm during the day, the nights were perfect. Humidity was merely a rumor. Dothan and some high school pals were prowling West Campus. The metallic orange to the west dazzled a little longer now that Daylight Savings Time had kicked in. After getting a college student to buy them a case of beer, the clan slammed can after can in the intermittent shadows. Earlier, a fraternity looking for recruits had picked them up at school. The boys had spent the latter afternoon watching skimpily clad girls mud wrestle at various frat houses. The drink they consumed at present was on top of what they had been given earlier at the event.

This was Round Up: the season when fraternities and sororities formally went to courting future pledges. In reality, this was an excuse to party. An alcohol soaked weekend that was indifferent to things such as, "being of age." This was the end of an era.

So, John David Dothan, a rock singer, aspiring fame and fortune; an artist of delicate sensibility, this is where he found himself on this particular April night in the latter nineteen-eighties: Buzzed and on top of the world, roaming a terrain that would never again be his own. But it was tonight.

"I need some smokes!" one of the clan announced.

"I'm fiending for a cigarette!" another concurred.

"I have to piss!" yet another sounded. This pronouncement was met with a unanimous holler.

This raucous crew exited off from the back streets that wound in and out of the tree shrouded nooks, hitting the main artery that cut through the middle of campus. As cars zoomed past, the boys swaggered into the aforementioned convenience store. After relieving himself, Dothan emerged out into the freshly darkened night. A red BMW convertible sat humming in the middle of the squat parking lot. A crowd of sycophants loitered. The longhaired singer recognized the prim driver. An amicable pop song, rising from its radio, filled the space.

"So hey JD, what's up with the band these days; where y'all playing next?" An acquaintance inquired.

"Oh man, you know we've been writing a ton lately," he prefaced, "and we're booked next on Sixth Street, in Joe's Generic Bar." Dothan sat on the hood of the running BMW.

"Joe's is cool, that means I can get in. They let underage in, don't they? That's what I've heard, anyway?"

"If not, I'll hand you a bag of mics. You can pretend you're a roadie."

"Hey, " a feminine voice called from behind.

Dothan sat, swiveling his head, confused.

"Yeah, you singer man; the hood!" The origin of the voice

was now pointing to the hood of her car.

Dothan, turned around and looked the girl square in the eyes. Perhaps the first time he had ever done so. Sitting behind the wheel, proud without arrogance, secure without conceit, how some might describe grace, sat Rachael Downs. Her soft brown hair blew in the wind, accenting her well-set jaw line and her olive skin.

Dothan lifted his skinny butt from the hood of the convertible and apologized, unconvincingly.

Rachel looked him up and down and cracked a wide smile. "It's alright. We're meeting some friends at a frat party. Why don't you join us?"

"Yeah?" he stated as he surveyed the landscape, "I know where y'all are going, we'll meet you there."

"Why walk? Why don't you hop in? Jump in the back, Alicia," Rachel ordered her friend, who was sitting shotgun. Dothan, was now sitting in the front seat, his long hair flapping in the wind as the Beamer accelerated.

The party was the usual fare of drunken fraternity types: basically, gangs of well-off white boys who were spoon-fed intolerance to anything remotely unlike themselves. The young singer would have served as an obvious target had it not been for the presence of a band. If there was anything Dothan was good at, it was talking fellow musicians into allowing him to sit in for a song or two, the official singer ignorant that he was about to be blown off the stage.

The eighteen-year old worked his magic. He was now a hero. The stunned band, returning to their set, felt a little awkward after such a superior performance: The official singer embarrassed; the rest of the band wishing they had Dothan.

Heralded as he made his way to the keg, he stumbled upon Rachael, his ride. "So, I guess you forget about the little people pretty fast?" she quipped, sarcastically.

Dothan was secretly flattered. "What are you talking about?" he shouted over the music. "I need to get a beer!" he called, signaling her towards the door.

The two convened outside the frat house, in a garden ensconced by giant, twisted live oaks; moonlight draping serpentine patterns across their figures and the moist grass.

"I really enjoy your music," Rachael commented.

"Thanks. That was a little sloppy, actually. I've sounded better."

"I know. I've heard you before."

"Before; where?"

"In the gym, at the talent show tryouts; a couple of weeks ago."

"You were there?"

"Yes, I was on the other side of the partition, working on stuff for the Youth Club fundraiser coming up."

"O…k…," Dothan was clueless.

"Yeah, I was really…well…really…moved. I know that sounds stupid."

Again, Dothan was secretly flattered. "No. I mean I'm glad you liked it. I've been told I sound best with just an acoustic accompaniment. It's awesome that that's how you first got to hear me!"

The arrogance of this was not lost on Rachael. "Acoustic? You'll have to fill me in. What does that mean?"

Dothan proceeded to explain the difference between acoustic and electric accompaniment. His sincerity excused his arrogance.

"You know, we have Government with each other?" she asked, accusingly.

"Yes, I know. I enjoy listening to your answers to Mr. Atkin's questions. You're by far the smartest person in the class."

This remark drew her further in. "We'll, I enjoy your opinions."

"What do you mean?"

"What do I mean? You have an opinion on just about everything. Or haven't you noticed?"

Dothan laughed at this observation. "No, I haven't."

"Well, you do. I like it. So many people our age just don't care or think about anything."

"I can't imagine not caring."

"Neither can I."

"How is it, having shared a class for the last three months, that we haven't ever said a word to each other before now?" Dothan asked, her flattery, and the booze, beginning to get to him.

"I don't know. But we're speaking now."

"Yes, we are."

～

"That'll be $6.49, sir," the convenience store clerk replied after Dothan asked for a pack of Marlboros.

The daydreamer was shocked back to reality. "$6.49? Jesus! A bit much, don't you think?"

"Taxes, sir."

"Here's ten. Keep it."

Dothan stepped out into the Austin night, his head cloudy, his heart full.

~

Back home along the coast, he arrived to an empty house. Jessica was on another one of her cruises or train trips. But loneliness was, in fact, what he was looking for. It suited his present mood and mindset.

There were numerous messages from Langhorne on the answering machine, the man rambling about some problem with a client. Dothan knew he needed to address the situation, but he was in no mood to deal with company issues.

The weekend was spent getting drunk and listening to music—a favorite past time. The only difference here was that the music he now listened to was his own. Tapes and homemade CDs of live shows and studio recordings lost to the world. He sat in his favorite chair, killing beer after beer, and gradually became enraptured with his own image. Verses and lyrics, long forgotten, were remembered with a myriad of emotions. But before passing out, Dothan could not help but feel that his life was a failure.

~

Come Sunday, after Langhorne had left several more desperate messages, he finally worked up the stomach to make the return call.

"Well, it's about goddamn time! What the hell took you so long? I've been calling for days!"

"Sir, I've been busy."

"Busy?"

"Yes, sir."

"Well look, JD, I'm having problems with that subcontractor over in Brazoria. I think he's getting cold feet—doesn't think the deal's gonna go through. Have you talked to that lobbyist I put you in touch with, the one that's friends with the chairman on the Appropriations Committee?"

"Yes, I have talked to him." Dothan was lying.

"Good!" Langhorne's tone calmed. "Fantastic, JD, fantastic. So…what did he have to say?"

"Nothing really, he wants to meet in person. I'm meeting him at his Austin office in the next couple of weeks."

"Next couple of weeks? What the hell's the delay?"

"It's the way things work, sir."

"Alright, all right. Did you at least go over some numbers with the man?"

"Numbers?" Dothan was caught off guard.

"Goddamnit, JD, I sent the file up to you more than a week ago! Haven't you looked at it yet?"

"Yes. I've looked at them. I can't remember anything off hand. It's all good. I've got it under control, sir."

"Good. I know I can count on you, JD." This uncharacteristic statement was followed by an odd silence. After a pause that seemed an eternity to Dothan, Langhorne continued, "Listen, JD. I tried breaching this subject with Jessica back at the beginning of this whole endeavor, and I expressed to her my reservations about you running as a Democrat. She was emphatic about it and it turned nasty, so I let it go. Look, I know that you and her are into that whole liberal thing—and I've been a Democrat all my life—but I'd be a liar if I told you that I wasn't concerned."

"Concerned about what, sir?"

"Concerned about you being in the minority party. And the way y'all crucified that Spencer fellow. And let's face it, JD the Democrats aren't what they used to be. Gay marriage and abortion—that ain't exactly the things I'm concerned about, you know."

"Sir, I can assure you that my party affiliation will not hurt me. I am making in-roads with both parties. With all the new freshmen reps., the possibilities are wide open."

"I don't give a shit about the possibilities; I want that job in Brazoria County— period!"

"Like I said, I've got it under control."

"Alright, alright…"

~

Dothan spent the beginning of the week meeting with potential business associates and county officials in Brazoria. Although at his core he loathed business, it was a welcome distraction from what was ailing him at the moment. From meeting to meeting he lied between his teeth, telling everyone involved exactly what each one wanted to hear.

Days later, when he left to return to the Capitol, he had everyone in the county excited about a project that, at that particular point in time, was merely a scheme in Langhorne's mind. Everyone, from the county judge to the county commissioners, as well as numerous subcontracting firms, were presently set in motion. Grandiose plans had been made.

chapter Eight

I.

"Harry, this is Reed, you have a minute?"

"Reed, how are you? How's the new session going; any trouble from that twerp that beat me?"

"Well, as a matter of fact, that's why I called, Harry, I'm chair on the Select Joint Committee…with him. The speaker was the one who appointed him. It's the Committee for Immigration Reform—vice-chaired by, get this, Ron Martinez."

"Martinez! That goddamn communist! What the hell is the speaker, the lieutenant governor, the damned governor for Christ's sake, thinking?"

"The governor is responsible. I think he believes it gives it legitimacy because he's a Democrat *and* Hispanic. Martinez is a sellout. I let him strut. I think he believes this will put him on the path to the Governor's Mansion at some point."

"So tell me about that little bastard, Dothan. What's his role? You wouldn't be calling if something wasn't fishy."

"Well, he's become Martinez's right-hand man; they office next door to each other, by the way."

"God almighty."

"I've got Logan in my corner, however."

"Logan?"

"Yes, you remember, Rachael Logan? State Senator out of Fort Worth?"

"You mean your brunette protégé'—out of Fort Worth?"

"Yes, that's the one," Reed confirmed, a squirm detectable in his voice.

"You gotta get that son-of-a-bitch Dothan, you've just got to."

"Yes, I know Harry. What he did to you was truly terrible."

"Truly terrible? Are you kidding me? He ruined my life, Reed. Ruined it!"

"Yes, I know Harry. How he won the election should go down in the Book of Revelation."

"He needs his balls cut off is what he needs!"

"I hate to ask this, but how are the divorce proceedings going?"

"I'm losing it all. I think about killing myself all the time now, you know?"

"The Lord will judge you harshly, Harry. Will Jane never forgive you? It's not like it was statutory rape."

"I don't think the one year in the age of that slut…I mean that girl…makes a difference to Jane. Look, I fucked it up. And it just wasn't that, 'one.' I couldn't control myself. I knew it was wrong, I just couldn't stop it; being with those girls made me feel like something other than a gray-haired old man—even if they were just prostitutes. But to be brought down by an out of work guitar player!"

"What's the status of the county district attorney? Is he still going to prosecute?"

"I'm not sure. I will die before I go to jail!"

"Harry, I'm going to look into Dothan. I promise you that. We've been friends for too long for me to let this go. I just have to be careful, Harry. You understand that?"

"Reed, you're the only friend I have left in the world. Please help me. At least give me the satisfaction of revenge."

"You have my word, Harry, as a fellow Republican, and more importantly, as a friend." The conversation now turned. "So how's the plan going otherwise, Reed?"

"Right on schedule; just as I foresaw. The governor is eating out of my hand, looking like a hero to Texas. Yet, at the same time, signing his own death warrant with regards to national office."

"And Martinez?"

"Perfect, though I must confess it was not entirely a part of my strategy."

"A useful idiot, you think?"

"Useful indeed. All the players have been put into motion. I regret you can't be a part of history directly. But you still can indirectly, Harry."

"Good. God Bless you Reed. You are the master at skull drudgery."

"I would prefer it, if you would use a more honorable description, in the future, my friend."

"I'm sorry, Reed. I didn't mean to offend you."

The two parties hung up their phones: Reed Jackson sat in his posh vacation home on Lake Travis while Harry Spencer was in his apartment with scarcely any furnishing.

Harry Spencer had been the incumbent Republican in the Texas House, the candidate that Dothan would have to beat. He had served for more than twenty years. But his House District, though for the past decade a Republican stronghold, had been tipping slightly blue. Still, any Democrat running in the general election would have an uphill fight. That is unless they knew how to fight dirty. And fighting dirty takes dirt.

Reed Jackson was the voice of the Christian right. He was also a former Army Lt. Colonel who had served alongside Harry Spencer in Vietnam. Although Reed Jackson was not a tolerant man, he was a loyal one. Or was he?

Believing that music had died with the King David administration, he would have innately despised a person like John David Dothan. Given the bonds he held with his former opponent, Dothan was anathema. Indeed, the former singer was a natural target for Reed's inborn urge to bully those who did not fit his narrow idea of humanity. Reed Jackson saw John David Dothan as a sitting duck.

II.

"So tell me Rachael, what do you make of this Dothan fellow?"

Reed Jackson inquired of his protégé while sitting in her spacious office on the fourth floor of the historic Capitol.

"What do I think of him?" she asked. She was seated behind her neat ornate desk. "I think he is a Democrat who believes the State owes something to everyone by taking it from those that produce it."

"Good observation—and very informed for having so little contact with the man. While we're discussing it, your admin told a member of my staff that Dothan had come calling unexpectedly the other day. Is that true?"

"Yes, Reed, he did."

"Can I ask the nature of his visit?"

"Of course, it was business. He knows I will carry the bill in the Senate—should we get that far."

"Does the man have a clue about policy? Wasn't he a singer or something?"

"I'm not sure. Maybe. I can't remember."

Rachael was slipping, and Reed Jackson detected it. "Well, I've taken up enough of your time. I must be going. Give Don and the kids my best."

"I will, of course. Thank you for coming by Reed."

Awkwardness lingered in Rachael's office. It was as if something, or someone, was still there. She needed air. She slipped out of her private office and into the foyer area where numerous staff members bustled about. Rachael vanished through a large open window. Once out on the open-air terrace, which sat just outside her office, she found that she could not shake the presence, it had followed her outside. With the late winter breeze rippling her clothes and blowing through her hair, she took a seat on one of the pink granite obelisks. Looking down on the crowded city, her thoughts and gaze settled upon the university; the tower visible through the chilly haze. The mind's eye took over and the dull gray cityscape below gradually took on the colors and smells of a long ago spring…

~

"Alicia, what did you think of him last night?" Rachael asked her fellow female companion, regarding the previous evening. She was lying on her bed, the phone between her shoulder and ear.

"Who?" Alicia asked from the other end.

"Who, who do you think? John David."

"Oh, I don't know; a little obnoxious."

"That's called confidence. You're mistaking confidence for conceit."

"I think it's the other way around, girl. You're mistaking conceit for confidence."

"Whatever. What are you doing? You sound distracted."

"I'm painting my toes."

"I need to do that, especially if I'm going to wear my red pumps tonight."

"So what are we doing exactly?"

"I thought we'd head out to campus and hit Roundup parties."

"Again, tonight?"

"Yeah, the dances are tonight."

"Dances, what do you have in mind?

"I'll call John David. Can you get a date? How about that guy you've been seeing?"

"Scott? I've already talked to him. I told him I'd let him know what was going on when I knew."

"Now you know."

"A little bossy are we? You should address your elders with respect."

The elders quip referred to the fact that Alicia was a freshman in college, where Rachael was only a senior in high school.

The convertible BMW wound its way through the tree-lined streets of West Campus—past the high dollar condos and apartments, the washaterias, pizza, and sandwich shops; towards the very edge, cradled only by a ridge that drops sharply off. There, tucked away in a tangle of trees, they headed to John David's apartment.

The three found Dothan smoking on the second story balcony of his two-story building. It was April and the days were getting longer and lusher. Dressed in slacks and a pink colored dress shirt, he looked the poised gentleman. Combined with the raven mane of unkempt hair and cowboy boots, he looked the enigma.

~

The clan raced through the night, party after party.

It was getting late, even by standards of the young. Two o'clock had come and gone. The frat house was thinning.

"Alicia, what's the status of the cabin?" Rachael inquired as the two stood waiting in line to use the bathroom.

"In Dripping Springs? Vacant. The folks are out of the country, who else would be there?"

"I don't feel much like going home. My parents think I'm spending the night at your house tonight."

"You want to ask the boys?"

"Yes, I would like that."

After finishing their respective business, the two young ladies went searching for their dates who had wandered off. Alicia, traversed the staircase; Rachael, the hall where the band had been playing; where the two had danced on and off for hours, until her feet hurt.

Bodies crisscrossed in front of her as she made her way across the old wooden floor. In the dispersing cigarette smoke the enigma appeared: part gentleman, part rebel. It was as if he had been waiting for her.

~

Alicia was at the wheel and Scott sat shotgun as the clan dashed towards Dripping Springs. With the city lights engulfed in the absolution of the country night, Rachael felt complete. There was no place she would rather be now. With high school soon to end, the anxiety of college pressing, this was a rare feeling. Staring out at the passing hills barely visible, but for the thin moonlight, the radio blaring, she placed her hand on Dothan's thigh. (Though the forty-something woman was sure that the two had kissed prior, this is the first time she actually remembered.)

They exited the highway, drove through a maze of back

roads and found the destination. A small house shone in the headlights of the BMW; it was more of a swanky cottage than backwoods cabin. Once inside, the posh contents confirmed this.

The refrigerator was raided for beer, the cupboard for wine. The boys negotiated a fire while the ladies excused themselves.

"Do you have anything out here for me to wear to bed, Alicia?" Rachael asked while putting her brown hair up in a chip clip.

"After watching *Arachnophobia,* my mother never keeps any clothes up here anymore. All there is are my father's horrible flannel shirts that he always wears—they're huge."

"That will work, as long as they're clean. I doubt it will survive the night."

"Girl, you are bad; so proper on the outside, what a shame," Alicia jested.

"I don't feel bad. In fact, I feel really good…actually."

Sitting on the couch, flipping channels, Dothan and Scott sipped the last remnants of a night well worn. Padding barefoot out of the master bedroom, where she and Alicia had prepared themselves, Rachael entered the den. "Well, what do we have here, a fire?" she remarked.

John David turned around from where he was seated on the couch and gazed at Rachael. The look in his eyes confirmed in her what she had already convinced herself would happen tonight. The flannel was so big that it hung to her knees; easily concealing the fact that she wore only panties underneath.

Alicia called for Scott from the master bedroom and signaled that the party was over.

After lighting a few candles, Rachael switched off the lights to the spare room where the two retired. Dothan sat on the bed, methodically removing his boots before undressing. Even in Texas, early April can be chilly. Rachel tucked herself under the covers, slipped off her panties, removed the chip clip and waited for John David.

He returned from the bathroom, with only his boxers on and joined her beneath the sheets. It was late—very late, almost morning. The two were tired, but determined. After much kissing and petting, the weight of Dothan was upon her. Rachael had been with two other men in her eighteen years—a conservative figure for the age.

Truth be told, Dothan had been with only a few more; also a very conservative figure for the age. Atop her, the two face-to-face, immune now to the cold, Rachael ran her fingers and hands across John David's naked back. She sighed.

"What?" he asked, insecurely.

"Nothing," she whispered, "your back…it's so smooth, so soft."

"Is that good?"

"Yes."

Drunkenness had caught up with both of them. Passing out, the two did not arise until the dull beams of dawn caressed the wooden room. In the cream color of early morning John David consummated the night. Moving atop her, Rachael, in her twilight state, took her lover in. It was perfect—neither uncomfortable nor awkward. For herself, when it was done…when they were done…she lay satisfied. Falling apart in exhaustion, the two returned to a state of sleep…

~

"Ma'am? Umm, Senator Dothan?" her admin, Caitlin, called from the office window.

"Yes?" Rachael answered, a little stunned. She was still sitting on the stone.

"Your husband is on the phone. Would you like me to tell him you will call him back?"

"No!" she declared. "I'll take it. Thank you."

~

Having purloined some pot from Jessica at an earlier date, tonight Dothan sat on his apartment sofa incredibly high. So high indeed, that he had begun to kill beer after beer in order to numb the paranoia. He was not a stoner by nature. In fact, he rarely touched the stuff. His present feeling of suspicion, fixation and utter fear would guarantee that it would be a while before he touched the stuff again.

What am I obsessing over? Everything and everyone. What to do about Langhorne; Tryphena; is Jessica cheating on me? And Martinez, what does he see in me? And Reed Jackson? What a weirdo. His mind raced until it rested at the thought of Rachael. Maybe it was the counter effect of the beers, but his paranoia began to subside.

A beautiful feeling presently overtook the man.

With a John Berry soundtrack playing low from the other room, Dothan sat at his desk with a pen and pad. A million thoughts and succinct memories had occupied his mind of late, but the absence of one annoyed him.

John David Dothan was not only an artist, but a craftsman as well. For all the anarchy of his outward appearance, the man had a gift of creating order out of chaos. This found its greatest expression in his poetry. Meter was his willing servant. Yet be it the weed, the beer, or the convoluted state of his being, his meter would not march. The syllables simply would not acquiesce under the gentle whip of technique. Giving up, he scribbled a few miscellaneous lines; subconscious lines that addressed that which plagued him:

> *Her cries upon climax,*
> *He could not recollect.*
> *He recalled a sound, but could not,*
> *For the life of him,*
> *Remember the tone…*
> > *The timbre…*
> > *The anima…*
> *He prayed that, upon blessed death,*
> *Her lone muse would revisit;*
> *Whispering those fateful notes.*
> *Those shapes in air, read by an ear.*

chapter Nine

I.

Rufus Taylor was dead.

Sitting in the hospital lounge, Tryphena tried to fill out the heap of paperwork that the hospital administrator had demanded she complete. She was in no state to deal with this and yet, she knew she had to. The weeks of suffering and the knowledge of the inevitable had cushioned her grief. Tryphena was more relieved than devastated; her innate mercy grateful that her brain-dead father would not languish as a vegetable.

She looked down at the black print on the screaming white paper, paralyzed pen in hand, and her thoughts raced: *Well, I guess Rufus finally found significance now that he's dead. The world will finally acknowledge that he was ever born. Only to punish those few left behind that loved him. The world will not let you grieve—that's a joke—something from a movie.*

109

Out of her pain and disgust, the woman let out a loud, single, mocking laugh. Her outburst caused visible discomfort to those sitting about her in the waiting area. Disregarding them, she returned to her thoughts. *I wish I had one of those Old West mourning outfits. That would shock all of these squares—showing up in a black lace dress and veil.*

God, how I hate the world. I really hate it, and all its formality and pretense. Those that make the rules have never suffered themselves, not a day in their life. They know nothing of life.

With this impulse occupying her brain, her mind pointed in the direction of a particular someone. Anger swelled up in her, quite irrationally. In her present state her instincts sought to place blame. All signposts signaled towards Representative John David Dothan. *What a spoiled, perverted white boy...* But before the thought could take full shape she stopped herself. *He's not that bad really. Kind of sad in a way. I owe him my livelihood. Rufus was a fuckup. His plight was his own doing. Oh, I don't know!*

Tryphena was in a state of shock.

She handed the clipboard to the nurse manning the area desk and vacated the hospital. Once outside in the cool air, she gathered her bearings. What she needed was a walk. With the sun setting, the night was getting chilly. After visiting her car, where she grabbed her coat, Tryphena took off down the sidewalk towards Rice University and the Museum District of Houston. Though rush hour was an issue, she did not let it inhibit her train of thought: *My livelihood? Yes, there are some nice people at the Capitol, but some of the legislators are disgustingly arrogant. They won't even look me in the eye—even acknowledge me. Even*

Dothan has changed. What is wrong with that place? And the committee chairs? All but Ron Martinez are so aloof that it's perverse. Nero's Rome had nothing on these amateur freaks!

Tryphena had walked several miles before turning back towards the Medical Center. Several times she tripped on the jagged sidewalk, which was broken intermittently by enormous tree roots. A moon, nearly full, shone through the intricately trimmed limbs of the giant live oaks that lined the car jammed streets.

She returned to the hospital and finished the mountain of paperwork.

Later, home at her Houston apartment, the daughter wasted no time in gathering up her father's things. It was strange, as if a geriatric had lived with her. There were little family and no friends that needed calling, only funeral arrangements to be made. *How to pay?*

Rufus Taylor was dead. He was forty-four.

II.

Dothan was adjusting to life at the Capitol. After a month of the House floor passing nothing but resolutions (the honoring or recognizing of respective local high school football teams, etc.), the House was finally taking up bills. It was mid-February and at last committees were beginning the arduous process of regurgitating legislation. The trouble was that the debate associated with these early bills was as boring as the past month and a half of resolutions.

Dothan was simultaneously happy and depressed with the completion of his committee appointments, which were announced at the end of January. Happy, because he had landed on the Culture Committee; depressed due to the anxiety accompanied by the fact that every one of the committees Langhorne insisted he request, were rejected by the speaker. Apparently, his auspicious appointment to the Select Joint Committee on Immigration Reform had used up his political capital.

But what occupied his mind the most was Rachael Logan. The SJC, (now the anagram for the Select Joint Committee on Immigration Reform), had entered a new phase. The committee had, through their findings, filed a "Recommendation." That Recommendation had been approved unanimously by the SJC. Now, two bills had been filed: Logan carrying the legislation in the Senate and Martinez in the House. Though Martinez was the recognized sponsor, the PR increasingly fell to Dothan with respect to the House. On the Senate side, Rachael Logan, the attractive brunette protégé of venerable Chairman Reed Jackson, was the obvious salesperson. Thus, in the media, the buzzword for the star legislation of this exclusive, somewhat controversial body was, 'The Logan-Dothan Bill'.

John David Dothan was making a name for himself despite himself.

This being the case, now that the bills had been filed and were in the pipeline, the frequencies of the meetings were fewer: spurious, once a week at best. In an environment as large as the Capitol Complex, it was simply impossible for Dothan to have much contact with Rachael outside of official business.

The good news was that Tryphena would be returning the first week of March. This whole situation had thrown Dothan considerably. Even given the fact that several part-time interns were now on staff, and while his admin, Pam, had proven to be a capable administrator, the freshman rep still needed his Chief of Staff.

When Monday rolled around, it was the weekly SJC meeting; an unusual day to look forward to, but a day Dothan looked forward to for obvious reasons. The meetings consisted of media prep to the members as well as what was needed to get the bills out of their respective chambers.

Around 10:00 p.m., the meeting was finally coming to a close. The tired faces peered at one another, relieved.

"I say we take this party over to the Austin Club!" Martinez declared.

This declaration was met largely with groans from the committee members.

"Ah, come on, Reed's not here—no one will care if you knock down a few!"

The majority of the committee called it a night, but four or five of the members surrendered to the vice chair's enthusiastic request. Both Logan and Dothan were game. The destination was within walking distance.

Vacating the Capitol, the party made their way down Congress Avenue towards the Austin Club: an old retired opera house that serves as the Tammany Hall of Texas politics. At 9th Street, the group took a sharp left.

In this 'Members Only' atmosphere the deals that shape this giant state are made. Under the muted light of the second floor, Martinez lead his company to food and drink. While the other members partook of the ample buffet, Logan and Dothan made their way to the long bar that stretched the length of an entire wall.

"What would you like to drink, Rachael?" Dothan asked, placing one black boot on the bar's brass foot rail.

"What kinds of wine do they have?"

"What kinds of wine do you have?" Dothan echoed to the bartender.

"Yes sir, I heard the lady," he nodded respectfully to them both, and then proceeded to rattle off a long list of grape-derived spirits.

"Cabernet—any…you pick," she directed Dothan.

"I'm not a wine drinker. I'll tell you what," he instructed the bartender with an air of play, "We'll defer to your professional opinion."

"Very well, sir. And for yourself?"

"Give me a Budweiser."

The bartender went about his duty. Rachael, clasping her purse, her arms crossed as if slightly uncomfortable, leaned towards Dothan. "Well, you certainly seem within your element. I thought you admired wine, as I recall."

"Admired? What does that even mean? Yeah, twenty years ago I liked wine. What the hell's wrong with you, you look like you're at a funeral or something, why don't you relax?"

"I guess I should go join the others."

"I would prefer it if you stayed here and admired a drink with me."

Rachael couldn't help but laugh. "You're such a smartass, John David. I'll stay."

The bartender placed two drinks before the couple.

"I still do admire wine," Dothan said, lifting his beer for a toast, "it just started hurting my tummy at some point and I decided the pleasure wasn't worth the pain."

"It might help if you drank only a glass or two, not the whole bottle," Rachael teased, obliging Dothan with his toast.

"I see you're still a smartass, as well."

"Wait, what do we toast to?"

"Uh…I don't know…how about the Logan-Dothan Bill."

"Don't get too enamored by the press, they can turn on you—and fast."

"I've been burned in the papers before."

"The music business isn't politics, John David. This game is more vicious than anything you can imagine."

"I know, I've had a taste. I've been knocked down, I can handle it."

"Well then, a toast…Logan-Dothan!" Through the chime of the two glasses a plea was heard from the dining room. "Will our two stars grace us with their presence?"

"In a moment!" Dothan shouted, bluntly.

"I think we're wanted," Rachael suggested.

"They can wait, can't they?'

"Remember your optics, John David."

"The two stars are discussing their next move—that's all," Dothan shouted back.

One drink turned into three, at least for Dothan. The rigorous schedule of the day had found the man with an empty stomach. The booze was taking effect. In this buzzed state, his emotional perceptions began to kick in. After nearly two months of reading legislation, what the artist would have detected by instinct had become blurred. For the first time, Dothan, through the course of his few drinks with Rachael, had identified her finely sculpted brown eyebrows; her dark brown eyes, not quite black. Coupled with the movement of her jaw in unison with her hands…it was coming back to him. Nothing had really changed, only the date on a calendar. The red lips juxtaposed against the olive flesh were unleashing an agony in the man. The perky breasts he remembered so well were now sitting firm on Rachael's chest behind a tight-fitted, red blouse. In a glance, his instincts, his emotions, his intellect, were all smashing into one another.

"I think we should join the others," Rachael said, grabbing her purse from the bar.

"Yeah, right," Dothan replied, disappointedly, stuffing a few dollar bills in the tip jar.

For the next hour the team ate, talked and drank. On the way back to the Capitol, Rachael walked ahead of Dothan, chatting with Martinez and the others.

Sauntering behind, his hands stuffed in his black pants, Dothan began to brood.

He waited in the parking garage for Rachael to arrive. While waiting, he popped open a bottle of cognac he had pulled from behind the seat of his '74 Ford.

The woman was now exiting the elevator. Placing the bottle on the back bumper, Dothan approached Rachael as she got into her tiny convertible Mercedes.

"Sweet ride."

"What!?" Rachael was startled.

"I said sweet ride."

"John David, you scarred me. Your voice is so powerful. You shouldn't sneak up on people like that."

"I wasn't sneaking up on you. I was just coming over to say goodnight. Tell you I enjoyed talking with you."

Rachael had gotten ahold of herself, and now felt a little self-conscious for reproaching John David. "Yes, I'm sorry. Silly me. Yes, I enjoyed our conversation as well, John David."

"So where to now?"

"Home. It's late. I don't wish to drink anymore. We have to get up tomorrow you know."

"How far is your apartment?"

"Oh, not far. I have a place up North Lamar."

"North Lamar. That's not too hip."

"I don't live somewhere because it's hip, silly. I live there because it's reasonable and not too horrible to get back and forth from. Of course the traffic in this city is just terrible. These liberals don't have a clue about city planning."

"So it's the fault of us liberals is it?"

"You're not really a liberal, John David. You're just not a Republican."

"Thank God." Dothan put his elbows on the door, leaning in towards her.

"You live just down South Congress, right?" she asked, a little uncomfortably.

"Right, just down the road. Would you like to see it? I've

got this awesome back balcony. It's littered with cigarette butts."

"Oh, how appealing. Phew, God your breath smells. What have you been drinking? I didn't see you hitting anything other than beer."

"Just a little cognac. Want some?"

"I don't think so, John David. And I don't think it's a good idea to visit your apartment tonight."

"Why?" he asked, innocently.

In that one syllable, John David's boyishness was unleashed. A million memories now fluttered in the woman's mind. For an instant, she thought she might. But that instant vanished like a popping ember.

"I have to go," she said, starting her car. "You have a good night, John David. I really am glad we've had this chance to reacquaint. I value our friendship."

Dothan knew that he had been beat. He could not challenge this rebuttal. Removing his elbows from Rachael's door, he gave a sarcastic salute. "Tell Reed Jackson I said hello."

"Although that wasn't sincere, I will tell him anyway."

"What?" Dothan staggered a little confused.

"I think it's time you found a pillow, John David. Can you drive or should I dial a cab?"

"No. I'm cool."

"I know you're cool, but are you OK to drive?"

"You really think I'm cool?" The boyishness was back.

"Yes, I do. But that has little to do with your ability to drive."

"I don't have that far to go. Don't worry."

"Alright, but let's hope I don't read about you in the paper tomorrow morning. I couldn't live with myself."

"I'm leaving. Goodnight."

Dothan turned and started walking back to his car. Rachael, concluding that it was hopeless to continue, put her car in gear and backed up. The intoxicated representative watched the light yellow convertible as it snaked its way up the exit ramp.

After a little drunken difficulty, he entered the cab of his truck. Fidgeting for the ignition key, he mumbled to himself, "She could've offered to take me home if she was that worried."

Dothan pulled out of his assigned space and vacated the nearly empty garage. The bottle of cognac fell from his back bumper, shattering on the garage pavement.

chapter Ten

Morning at the Capitol was getting earlier and earlier. It was now not unusual for Pam to open the office no later than 7:00 a.m. The young, pudgy woman's morning routine consisted of visiting the bathroom, grabbing a cappuccino from the cafeteria, and then swinging by the House mailroom. Representative Dothan's box was always stuffed with invitations to events. On this particular dawn there was an invitation of particular interest.

Dothan's daily habit was strolling into the office no earlier than thirty minutes before the House floor convened; this time being arbitrary, and such was the time of his arrival. In short, Dothan had no pattern. Today Dothan would not show up until nearly noon. He arrived both hung over and troubled. Pam followed her boss back to his office. Her boss threw himself down into his large leather chair and looked in disgust over the scattered contents of the desk before him. "This place is a fuckin' mess!"

"I'm sorry sir, we'll get on cleaning it up ASAP."

"Is there a reason why there are a ton of newspapers everywhere?"

"You requested that I not throw any of them away, sir." Pam answered, robotically.

"I did?"

"Yes, sir."

"Well, throw them away!"

"All of them, sir?"

"Yes!" No sooner had this edict escaped his lips, than Dothan began rummaging through the piles of newspapers. "Wait, there's an article in the *Statesman* about Rachael and me. Find it and then pitch the rest."

"Yes, sir."

"What's the deal with Tryphena?"

"It hasn't changed since she called, sir. She'll be back in about a week."

"Good. Is there anything else? I need to go over the agenda for today."

"Yes, sir. There is some mail I need to go through with you briefly."

After sifting through the bulk of the mail, Pam arrived at the invitation of particular interest. "And this is an invite to a dinner at Eddie V's restaurant, here in downtown Austin."

"What's it for?"

"It's being held by Texans for Smart Immigration Policy or 'T-SIP.' It's to congratulate the committee for their hard work this session."

"Really? A little early for congratulations…isn't it? And

I guess they're happily ignorant of the centuries old rivalry between UT and A&M."

"Uh, yes I suppose so, sir. Should I RSVP?"

"Of course! When is it?

"It's this Friday, sir."

"This Friday! Kind of short notice—wouldn't you say?"

"Yes, sir."

"Anything else on the schedule that night?"

"No, sir."

"Well, send in the RSVP. Is that all?"

"Yes, sir."

Pam vacated his office, closing the representative's door behind her. Dothan was relieved. He found Pam irritating.

"Jesus Christ, she's like a chubby Peppermint Paddy," he confessed out loud in a muted voice, fearing Pam might hear him.

This news, however, turned the man around. The morning had been a headache of regret. Now the rest of the week would be one of hopeful possibility.

~

Dothan was standing outside Eddie V's smoking a cigarette with the valet guys when Reed Jackson pulled up in his black Lincoln Town Car. Rachael Logan emerged from the front passenger door. This struck him negatively.

"Good evening Representative Dothan, I didn't realize you smoked," Reed Jackson commented while putting on his black overcoat.

"I don't…really. I was just enjoying the company of my new friends."

Reed was clearly offended by this spectacle. "Come Rachael, allow me to escort you inside."

"Well, thank you Reed, you're such a gentleman." Before entering the establishment, Rachael turned towards John David and remarked, "You shouldn't smoke Representative Dothan; it really is a bad habit all around. You're too valuable to our cause." Reed and Logan vanished inside.

"Well pardon me all to hell," Dothan apologized in his best John Wayne impersonation. With his boot sole he stamped out the cigarette. "Well fellas, you see what I have to contend with this wonderful evening—wish me luck."

"Good luck!" The valets echoed with bravado.

Within the low-lit establishment Dothan strutted well camouflaged. Dressed completely in black, with the exception of a blood red tie, he was nearly indistinguishable from his surroundings. And yet his confident demeanor belied his homogenous presence. Table after table turned with a strange fascination at his passing.

Behind a set of mahogany French doors awaited his destination.

"Well there he is! Fashionably late as always JD!" Martinez announced to the small banquet room. Rising from the long dark table, the Vice Chair squeezed his way between the rows of back-to-back chairs, lining the two long tables. "My friend, I'm so glad you are here. Come, there are some people I would like you to meet—big donors," Martinez said, nudging his leading man in the ribs.

Speaking with the lobbyists for T-SIP, Dothan was disengaged; his pleasantries masked his wandering eye.

"Would it be possible to get a picture of you with Senator Logan?" One of the lobbyists asked.

"Of course. I haven't been able to locate her, however."

"I'm right here Representative," Rachael replied from behind. She slipped her arm through John David's and nestled up to his side; she directed the scene.

"I think this is a good shot. What do you think, is the lighting adequate?"

"What are you the paparazzi?" Dothan muttered lowly.

"Smile, like a good show poodle," Rachael muttered in retort. With pictures snapping, she leaned further into her co-star. "You smell like cigarettes, John David."

"Sorry, Mom."

"That'll do!" The lobbyist enthusiastically declared, having caught not a word of the discourse unfolding before him. Breaking off, Rachael excused herself, making her way across the room. Chairman Jackson stood conversing with a party of devotees and lingered there until dinner was served.

With the party enjoying the feast, in between bites of fish, steak and sips of wine, all conversation turned to the business at hand.

"So tell me Chairman Reed, what prompted you to take such a backseat on such an important piece of legislation?"

Reed puffed up and answered in the haughty manner, which was his custom. "I wouldn't say that I'm taking a back seat. The fact is, I have tremendous confidence in the members of our committee— particularly Senator Logan and Representative Martinez."

"What about JD Dothan?" Another member of T-SIP asked from the end of the table.

"Representative Dothan serves a purpose."

"You mean the PR?" the man continued.

Rachael Logan, sensing the awkwardness swirling about her, interjected, "My goodness, is this an interview or a dinner party? I must say gentleman, I thought T-SIP was a political action committee, not a school of journalism."

The table laughed, having been disarmed by *the* Lady Senator.

Dothan sat silent mulling over, in his slightly intoxicated brain, a million obnoxious retorts to the stuffy chairman.

Conversation took independent flight, numerous pockets sparking up here and there.

Dothan was slamming beer after beer. He sat gazing over at Rachael, who wore a red dress; her toned olive arms naked at the shoulders. The man's romantic instincts were eating into his soul.

A cell phone started ringing, interrupting the flow of discussion. It was silenced. It rang again, and again. Reed Jackson, rising from his chair, excused himself.

Perhaps a half-hour passed before the chairman returned. Signaling to Martinez from the helm of the table, the two began, what appeared to be from Dothan's angle, a rather heated discussion. Reed Jackson left again.

"JD!" Martinez half shouted.

"Yes?" Dothan answered, startled, as was the rest of the dinner party.

"Would you mind taking Senator Logan home? She arrived with Reed and he has to go, as well as myself. I would be grateful."

"Of course!"

"That's not necessary, my car is at the Capitol. I can walk back, Representative Martinez," Rachael said. She noticed the alarming nature of both Ron and Reed and inquired, "May I ask, what is the emergency?"

"Just an issue the chairman and I have to attend to. Sorry for the dramatics."

Turning towards Rachael, Dothan insisted, "Senator, it's supposed to freeze tonight; there may even be a chance of rain."

"Yes, yes my lady, please, the chairman and I really insist," Martinez confirmed.

~

Drizzle accumulated on Dothan's front windshield as he and Rachael waited for his ancient heater to begin warming the pick-up's cab.

"Shit, I left my coat in Reed's car," Rachael regretted, as she rubbed her bare arms.

"Here, put on my jacket." While assisting her, Dothan's hands repeatedly brushed against Rachael's soft flesh.

"So where to now?"

"Where to now?" Rachael repeated, confused.

"Yes, where to now? Do you just want to go home? It's only a little after ten."

"We have to get up tomorrow, John David. I think it would be wise to call it a night."

"Do you want to hit 6th Street or downtown—maybe go dancing?"

"Are you crazy? I'm not really dressed to go out to a bar or club."

"You look great! What the fuck are you talking about?"

"I appreciate your approval but…what would everyone think?"

"Think? Who cares? It's just the two stars out being stars."

"John David, this isn't Hollywood. Bad behavior doesn't translate into ratings—particularly not for a Republican."

"Look, let's grab one or two drinks, and then I'll take you back to the Capitol to get your car. Or, I can take you home and drive you to work in the morning," Dothan concluded with a boyish grin from ear to ear.

Rachael looked accusingly at him. "OK, I surrender. Where to have this drink, or two?"

"Really…you want to go?"

"Yes, John David, I want to go. Where to?"

Dothan pulled out from Eddie V's. The drizzle had stopped. Though Friday night, the weather had rendered the streets of downtown Austin easy to maneuver.

"I really like this truck John David," Rachael commented sitting up with perfect posture.

"Really, you really like it?" Dothan asked, perking up like a little boy.

"Yes, really, I like it. It's cool. Why are you so surprised by my receptivity?"

"I guess because it's foreign to me."

Rachael patted his shoulder in a sort of comforting, maternal fashion; Dothan, looking adoringly over at her in his passenger seat, remarked, "You look so cute in my suit coat. You have no idea how cute you look!"

"Watch the road John David. Watch the road."

The music of the club thumped. The two tried dancing but Rachael's pumps were not up for it. Neither recognized most of the music being played. Dothan felt it necessary to visit the DJ. He believed this meeting to be unsuccessful. Drinking at the bar, a song started that the two remembered well (and it had not been requested by Dothan.) It was immediately recognizable.

"Awesome!" Rachael yelled as she shot up from her vodka and tonic.

"'Just Like Heaven!'" Dothan bellowed, slamming his scotch.

Immersed in the swirling lights of the dance floor, the two legislators tried hard not to embarrass themselves. It did not matter. Once the tap of 'times gone by' is shifted on, it is difficult to shut off. Moving his body toward her, he clasped Rachael around the waist. The two figures swayed and bounced, bounced and swayed.

One or two drinks, turned into three, then four, and so on. But time had flown and it was time to call it a night. The two were hot and sweaty. Sitting in Dothan's truck, the cold evening air gnawed into their bones.

"God, this is a cool truck John David, but I sure wish you had a better heater," Rachael commented, her teeth chattering.

"Yeah, that's kind of the trade-off for something this old. Here, let me warm you." Reaching over, he began rubbing the sleeves of his coat. Rachael promptly embraced John David; his face now buried in her hair, his lips within whispering distance from her ear. "Your teeth are chattering," he murmured.

"Shut up, silly. I'm freezing," Rachael playfully retorted, looking slightly up into John David's eyes. A car horn blared from behind them! Startled, Rachael immediately became recalcitrant. Dothan, returning to his upright position behind the wheel, took on a dour expression; halfway knowing something like a horn blowing was par for the course.

"We have to get out of here, John David!" Rachael pleaded as the horn sounded again.

Dothan punched the gas and the car flew out of the parking garage. "Jesus Christ, John David, slow down. We don't want to get pulled over. I know you've had too much to drink, as have I."

"I've got a pistol in the glove box," he said in a creepy fashion.

"Are you trying to scare me—what on earth for? Do you have a Concealed Hand Gun License?"

"No."

"You drive to the Capitol, park in a reserved spot, and you don't have a CHL? You are crazy!"

"Not really. I'm just not going to jail—ever!"

"What does that mean?"

"Nothing, I'm being stupid," he answered. Realizing he might be blowing it, Dothan collected himself. "So, what would you like to do? I still haven't shown you all those cigarette butts on my balcony."

"You really shouldn't be smoking, John David. However, I would like to see all those cigarette butts on your balcony," Rachael said, nervously.

"Really?" The boyishness had returned.

"Yes. I'm too drunk to attempt driving home, and your place is much closer than mine. I think we should just get off the road."

~

"Here we are," Dothan said as he switched on the den light to his apartment.

"OK, I'm reserving judgment," Rachael toyed while observing the den.

"You want some wine or something?" he asked from the kitchen.

"Or something…how about water?"

"Come on, just one more. Let me admire a glass of wine with you."

"You're pushing your luck mister," Rachael jested.

With wine glasses in hand, the two sat on Dothan's sofa. Delving into his considerable CD catalog, one of the only creature comforts he had brought with him from home, U2 now echoed lowly from the stereo.

"So what should we toast to?" Dothan asked.

"How about the great unknown."

"The great unknown?"

"Yes," Rachael confirmed, adjusting her posture into a perfect right angle, "the great unknown…who would have ever foretold our reintroduction to one another?"

Dothan was captured, and could only repeat, raising his glass, "The great unknown!"

The two glasses chimed with the subtle music. Rachael yawned. "It's time to turn in John David."

"It is?" he asked in a fatalist tone.

"It is. So what are the sleeping arrangements?"

"Well, I can sleep here on the couch. You can sleep in my bed?"

"You are so silly."

"I am?"

"I don't mind sharing a bed with you John David, I've done it before. We're both drunk. We're both married. We both have to go to work in the morning. I trust you."

Dothan was sitting somewhat bewildered.

"My only question John David is: do you have anything I can take my makeup off with?'"

"I have soap."

"That will do. Anything I can change into, a t-shirt?"

"Yes!"

Although Dothan had cranked up the apartment heater before retiring, his Spartan bedroom was freezing. Retrieving numerous blankets from the closet, he did his best to keep his guest comfortable. Laying in darkness, the two bodies inevitably moved towards their mutual warmth.

Dothan wore only his underwear; Rachael, her panties and a t-shirt of Dothan's. Face to face they lay.

"I've thought about this countless times through the years," Dothan said into the shadow that was Rachael's face.

"Oh John David, you're such a romantic," she whispered back, surrendering her lips to his. Kissing holds allure in three phases of one's life: In youth, before the magic of sex is experienced; before the dullness of marriage takes grip; and then, after the magic of sex has ceased, but the dullness of marriage remains. It is a peculiar art form that is the sole domain of lovers.

The two exhausted legislators drifted asleep. From the den, the music continued to play. After U2, the stereo switched disks to Tommaso Albinoni's *Adagio in G Minor*.

~

The silver of winter morning had just barely begun to distribute its shade about John David Dothan's bedroom, when Rachael Logan began to wake. This jostling of the mattress caused her counterpart to rise as well.

"What time is it?" Dothan asked, reaching for the glass of water at his bedside.

"Time to get up. Time to address reality John David."

"What? What are you talking about?" Dothan asked, sitting up.

Rachael was sitting on the edge of his bed, dressing. "What am I talking about? I'm talking about reality John David. Something you apparently have difficulty with."

"What? What is wrong with you? We haven't done anything. There's no reason for you to be this way. We are innocent!"

"Are we? I remember kissing you. I don't remember anything else."

"I can tell you that that is all that happened!"

"I have your word, as a gentleman? Why are you getting so defensive?"

"Jesus Christ, go check yourself in the bathroom if you don't believe me! And fuck you for believing I would be capable of…that!"

"I'm sorry, I…I…I have to go." Rachael rose from the bed. A thought that had lingered in her head for some time, now forced itself to the forefront. "Have you given any thought to what will occur when the press delves into our mutual pasts and discovers we've been together?"

"That was a quarter century ago."

"That doesn't matter, my love. The press, if so inclined, can find out anything about anyone."

"OK, but nothing happened last night." Dothan was seized by her image before him. "But God, you are so beautiful. Only a fool would pass up an angel like you. I am a fool."

"No John David, you're a gentleman—despite yourself."

"Would you like me to call you a cab?"

"You read my mind."

"I understand."

Dothan remained inside his apartment as Rachael made her cab. It was not lost on the man that she had referred to him as, "my love."

chapter Eleven

Reed Jackson and Ron Martinez had checked in at the La Copa Hotel, not far from Miller International Airport. The weather in McAllen was a bit sultry on this, the first of March. Conversation on the flight from Austin was minimal. Now, as each withdrew from their respective rooms, they hurried to meet in the lobby of the hotel.

"When we get to the press conference, follow my lead," the chairman instructed his second in command as the two hastily made their way to their rental car.

"Are you sure you know how to play this, Reed?" Martinez asked. He gazed out the window at the profusion of palm trees.

"I've never been so certain of anything in my life, Ron."

The drive to the press conference was not far. A tranquil blue sky reflected across the convention center's long rectangular pond, as the black Lincoln Town Car pulled into a parking lot filled with television vans. Inside the convention center, the two traveling companions were lead to a small event room. The room was swarming with reporters, journalists, congressman, FEMA, Homeland Security and the like. A long table, with numerous microphones, sat at the back of the room.

Reed Jackson wasted no time in ingratiating himself to his colleagues from the federal government. Martinez followed behind like an obedient dog.

After assembling at the back table, the array of officials and their enforcers readied themselves. The press conference began.

The reason for this makeshift event was a briefing by the Feds regarding the school bus bombing; the event that had instigated the creation of the Select Joint Committee on Immigration Reform. Thus far, very little in the way of progress had been made. This press conference would confirm this.

"Well sir," a reporter inquired from a Homeland Security official, "you keep contending that this was an act of sabotage committed by any one of numerous drug cartels…but none of the evidence suggests this. In fact, all of the major syndicates have come out in condemnation of this act. Why do you still contend that this was done by the drug lords?"

Reed Jackson, who sat on the end of the panel, interrupted, "Our friend from the federal government quite simply does not know, nor do any of his associates from the usual alphabet soup. The bottom line: it probably is one or more of the cartels, angry about the recent federal immigration law that interrupts, possibly destroys, their near monopoly on human trafficking. If so, they have indeed graduated into an insidious industry—what our president refuses to acknowledge—terrorism!"

Martinez, who sat in the crowd, listened with nervous amazement. Only a moment ago Reed Jackson was personally praising these men. Now he was publically condemning them.

The chairman continued, "For nearly ten years, I sat on, and then chaired, the Texas Legislature's division of Homeland Security. The reason I resigned was simple: from our briefings from the Feds, my lasting impression was one of luck. How lucky we are as a nation to be as safe as we are with these incompetents running things from D.C.?"

The room was stunned by this admonishment. An agent from the FBI tried breaking in, but Reed cut him off, "Leave us! Just leave our great state of Texas! Haven't you hurt our people enough? Let our Attorney General and Texas Rangers figure this out! I assure you they would do a better job!"

Reed Jackson, the tall, pigeon chested, white-haired, seventy-year-old state senator, abruptly vacated the room. The vast lobby of the convention center filled with interested onlookers as he charged off with an uncanny display of purpose.

Martinez followed behind and the two left the building to a round of cheers and cries to "Secede!"

The drive back up to Austin was not nearly as meditative as the plane ride down to McAllen. Martinez wiped the sweat from his forehead with a handkerchief; his adrenaline was still pumping. "McAllen is my district Reed; it's my backyard. I wonder if your theatrics may not have caused more harm than good?"

"My friend," Reed replied from behind the wheel, "you worry far too much. I have been doing this for a long time. How old are you Ron?"

"Forty-nine."

"Forty-nine," Reed echoed. "In twenty years you will understand."

"Understand what?"

"Once time has exhausted your ambitions, your true power awaits."

"What do you mean?"

"I'm doing this for everyone *but* me. I'll be dead soon. I have a number of ailments. I've lived longer than nearly anyone in my family tree."

"Is there something you haven't told me? Do you have cancer or something?"

Reed laughed, then answered, "No, I haven't got cancer, Ron." His cell rang from his coat pocket.

"Who is it?" Ron asked, as Reed stared at his phone screen.

"Harry."

"Harry Spencer?"

"Yes, Harry Spencer."

"Are you going to answer it?"

"Not now. I'll call him back later."

"I don't like it that he is in the know; that Harry Spencer is a volatile man."

"No doubt, he is a loose end. That's why I keep him close to the vest."

"Have you kept him abreast of things since this past fall?"

"He is ignorant of your involvement, if that's what you are asking."

"Good. A man that perverse cannot be trusted. It still astonishes me that you, of all people, could be friends with him."

"The inertia of time betrays even righteousness. It's not just Marines that possess a brotherhood. Harry and I survived things that men of your generation will never know."

"I know you to be a true patriot, Reed."

"A patriot, or a traitor?"

"No one could deny your love of country. It is not your fault that the nation has been led astray."

Reed changed the subject, "Any news from your contact in the Valley?"

"Nothing since our final meeting, two weeks ago."

"So we are square?"

"Yes."

"Can we trust *him*?"

"We've had this discussion before. Yes, we can trust him!" Martinez retorted.

"So he has vanished."

"As he should!"

"Yes, as he should."

The night was setting in. The Black Lincoln shot northward towards Austin. After San Antonio, the darkness between it and the Capitol City—the darkness that the two travelers knew as rote—had vanished.

"I still can't get used to the fact that this route is now nothing but lights. I remember when it was darkness from UT to Southwest University," Martinez commented.

"Yes Ron, I recall. Our beloved state is the magnate of

opportunity…for the world. The reason we do as we do."

"A justification, Reed?"

"Indeed."

II.

Tryphena had returned with little fanfare. The workload was so immense by now that there was little time to celebrate. Dothan, retired repeatedly to his back office, leaving the door shut. From under the door, the foreign sounds of Joy Division emanated from his computer. Pam, as a testimony to her artlessness, said it sounded like devil worshipping music. Tryphena preferred it to the industrial noise of one of Dothan's other favorites: Killing Joke; or worse, the blatantly offensive Sex Pistols and Dead Kennedys.

Tryphena was adjusting to life at the Capitol in hyper-mode. When she had left, a month ago, not much in the way of stressful work was happening. Now, House bills were stacking up. She was in the process of acclimating her staff to the fact that she was in charge, and not Pam. Pam was adjusting as well. This office of all females was in a state of flux. Everyone was uncomfortable. Dothan was disengaged.

The mail was stacking up as well. The lone man of the office simply refused to address it. Pam, in her frustration, began automatically to RSVP in the negative. Day after day the stack of unopened letters grew in stature. Tryphena, absorbed in the duty of reviewing bills, gave the go-ahead to just begin opening everything on behalf of Dothan—no matter how private.

Most of the articles were junk, as is usually the case with mail. A few, however, were of the variety as to raise flags.

"Ms. Taylor?" Pam called from the front desk.

"I've asked you to please refer to me as Tryphena, Pam. What is it?" she answered from her office.

"There are a couple of pieces of mail that I think you should see."

"What are they?" Tryphena asked approaching Pam's desk.

"Well, ma'am, one is a document from the Texas Ethics Commission. The other is a letter that appears to be personal in nature."

"From whom?"

"From Senator Logan, ma'am."

Tryphena retired, with the mail in question, to the privacy of her office.

The letter from Senator Logan was indeed personal in nature. And though brief, it was disturbing:

John David, as I have told you on numerous occasions, I am grateful that we have had the opportunity to reacquaint. When I say that I am so proud of you for what you have accomplished, I am being sincere. It is not meant to be patronizing. You are the most talented man I have ever known. You deserve success and happiness.

After last Friday night, I have been in a state of conflict. Seeing you again after all these years can't help but open up old hopes, and yes...old wounds. We are all of us mortal, and as such, suffer the weaknesses of our condition.

With that, I regret to inform you that our relationship will, from henceforth, be strictly professional. There will not be another, "last Friday night."

You have so much to offer. This is for the best. We cannot jeopardize the ends of our work. We are both married, and have followed the path found in God's plan. It is a covenant we cannot break. I know that you will be angry, but in time you will know that I am right. Love always, Racheal.

Tryphena was shocked. With all that had happened she had forgotten about the photograph in the volume of Shelley; she had forgotten about the, "Rose of my Memory."

I knew it! I knew that there was something about to happen. Oh, Rep. Dothan, you are such a fool. How did you get this far in life? What should I do with this letter? Pam has already opened it. Fuck! Pam! Now she knows something is going on between you two! How should I let him know? It is opened. Fuck! I'll have to think of something – he has to know what Rachael is saying. I wonder what happened last Friday night? Wait a minute; this is dated almost two weeks ago. What was on the calendar that Friday?

Tryphena did not know how to juggle Pam. First off, she did not trust her. Pam was odd, and always angling to make herself look more important than she actually was. Secondly, it was none of her business what Dothan did in his private life. To possess such knowledge was dangerous, both for the representative and Pam—but how to deal with it?

Tryphena's solution to the 'Pam' situation was to play it down.

The second piece of mail in question was the document from the Texas Ethics Commission, which was a more pressing issue. In the state of Texas, when one decides to run for public office, they must first file with the Ethics Commissions, designating someone: Treasurer. In most instances it is the spouse or a friend of the candidate; it really doesn't matter. A treasurer's function is to report all campaign donations, as well as monies paid out from the campaign. These reports are broken into specific timeframes, congruent with the due date for filing them. Dothan's designated treasurer was his wife, Jessica. According to this document, Jessica had failed to report donations for the final fundraising period of December 31. The deadline for reporting these funds was over a month ago. Dothan was in danger of incurring an ethics violation for this oversight. While in reality, it was nothing more than a simple mistake. It could prove to be a negative issue if one were to have an opponent in the future. This was something that Tryphena had to address immediately.

There was no need to waste her time with Jessica. Tryphena knew that any questions on her part would be construed as a reproach, and thus, an attack on Jessica's integrity. As Chief of Staff, she decided to handle it herself. Logging onto the Ethics Commission website, she began to do a little research. The past reports for her boss revealed little in the way of confusion for Tryphena, as they were cut and dry. Jessica had, heretofore, done her duty well.

Out of curiosity, she decided to look at the reports of

others in the legislature. Since these reports were public record, all that was needed was a name. For an hour or so Tryphena sifted through different representatives' and senators' campaign financial information; mainly in an attempt to discover how much money they respectively had in their war chests. When examining Senator Reed Jackson's reports, a company name filed under, "expenditures" struck her as familiar. *But where have I seen this name before?* She repeated the name over and over, trying to jog her memory. *"Victory Ballot!" "Victory Ballot!" Where did I see that name? …Ah ha! "Victory Ballot!" That was the name on the caller ID when I got the call from Warren Jenkins about this job opening!*

She raced back to Dothan's information on the Ethics Commission site and sifted through the campaign consultant/management information; she found only the company title of "Jenkins and Clark Inc." Tryphena now did a search on all the names involved. *Voila! 'Victory Ballot!' is Warren Jenkins. Is that unusual? Or just peculiar? I wonder if Rep. Dothan knows that Reed Jackson and Warren were, or are, business associates?*

This had been, if not a momentous day, an odd one.

It was getting late. Dothan was still on the floor around 10:00 p.m.

It was time for Tryphena to cut everyone loose; time to address the letter that she had given Pam permission to open. "Ya'll can go," she informed the staff. "Oh and Pam, before you call it a night, would you mind coming into my office?"

"Yes, ma'am."

Once in the office, Tryphena tried to feign an air of

triviality. "Regarding the ethics stuff, we were late on our campaign report. Hopefully, I can get the information filed and get us in the clear. We don't want to piss this agency off. They can make problems for us. Regarding the other thing…I'm sure that Representative Dothan is already aware of this. I'm sure there is nothing to it. The two parties have had political dealings with one another in the past. I think there was some bad blood—I'm not sure. I wouldn't concern myself with it any further. But thanks for going through all that mail."

"Yes, ma'am." Pam sat stone-faced. Her robotic body language was impossible to read. "Will that be all? I am really tired and we have a busy day tomorrow."

"Yes we do. That will be all. And again, thank you."

Tryphena was getting paranoid. The environment of the Capitol can do that.

∼

Things were so hectic that it took a couple of days to pin the representative down in order to discuss the mail in question. Regarding the letter from Rachael Logan, she decided since it was already opened, to lay it out with other pieces of opened mail of no significance. Perhaps it would lay to rest any suspicion he might have that others were aware of it. It appeared to work, as he did not mention it at all. However, Tryphena would make sure that the Ethics Commission issue was discussed.

"We need to talk." Tryphena addressed Dothan in his office first thing in the morning.

"About what? I have to get my act together for the floor today. You know how I hate not knowing what's going on. Having to distil bills from the author while they are at the mic is no way to legislate." (The truth was that work was a distraction from thinking of Rachael.)

"This is important."

"Ok, what's up? Close the door."

Tryphena closed the door and sat down. "How do you know Warren Jenkins?"

"My consultant? Well, if I remember correctly, he contacted me after discovering that I had filed to run. Why?"

"Nothing unusual about that I suppose, just a guy looking for business. However, looking into your Campaign Finance Report, which by the way is late, I came across an interesting piece of information."

"The Ethics Commission is on my ass? Fucking Jessica!" Dothan remembered his manners, "I'm sorry, Tryphena, excuse my language."

"It's alright, sir. I don't mind."

"So the report is wrong or late, is it?"

"Late—a month or so."

"So what is the interesting piece of information?"

"Were you aware that Warren's company, Victory Ballot shows up on Reed Jackson's reports?"

"Reed Jackson?"

"I didn't think so."

"I don't understand. What does it mean?"

"Nothing, probably, it's just strange that he never told you.

When he contacted me…"

"Warren contacted you? I think I remember him telling me he had placed an ad at U of H."

"Actually, he contacted me and told me about this gig that was opening up—your gig. I had put the word out through the Poli-Sci Department that I wanted a job in the State Legislature. That's where Warren got my information. I don't remember an ad. It was before you won, actually. Which is why I was at Peck's that night…the night you won."

"Hmm, I'll have to ask him…but strange…very strange."

"It would appear that way, sir."

"Jesus, how long have we known each other?

"Since November."

"Will you call me JD? You sound like Pam."

Tryphena laughed.

chapter Twelve

Langhorne was back, back from Washington D.C. He was not happy as he sat there in Dothan's office, while Tryphena made the long trek from the underground extension to the Capitol proper. She exited the second floor elevator and made her way through a swarm of lobbyists, finally handing a note to an available House Page. Not too long afterward, Dothan emerged from the House Chamber with his hair and suit disheveled.

"Jesus, JD, what happened to you? You look like you got dressed in the dark."

"What, am I messy?"

"Very."

"I want to pull my hair out after arguing with that fucking asshole from DFW."

"I was watching you on the House broadcast from the office. You tore that guy up!"

"I don't think reason and superior arguments matter to some of these people. They're egomaniacs."

"I'm not going to argue with that."

The two entered a crowded elevator.

"So Langhorne's in my office. Is Jessica with him?" Dothan whispered to Tryphena as they stood pressed tightly up against one another.

"Yes," she said, rolling her eyes, "to the first question, and no to the second."

"How is he? I mean, what's his disposition?"

"He's always an asshole." She mouthed these last two syllables.

"I'm not going to argue with that."

The two bolted out of the elevator with lightning speed. Dothan was a fast walker—very fast. Tryphena was the only one who could ever keep up with him.

Dothan entered his headquarters with an odd sense of confidence and foreboding. He learned news regarding Langhorne's Brazoria project; news he had withheld from his father-in-law. He entered his private office; Tryphena shut the door. The two men were alone.

"I'm sorry I'm late, sir. The floor can be like watching paint dry—then wham—all of a sudden, a lively discussion sparks up."

"I've been waiting here for half an hour, JD." Langhorne's tone was morose.

"Yes sir, I'm sorry about that. What can I do for you today?"

"Jesus Christ JD I'm not a goddamn lobbyist. Talk to me like a human being." The boss was back.

"What's up?"

"I've been in Washington. What the hell's wrong with that place?"

"Is that an actual question? What are you referring to, exactly?"

"Used-to, you could bullshit or bribe your way out or into something. These agency-types, they're like goddamn Soviets!"

"Are you referring to your lobbyist fellow from the TBA, the guy who was supposed to have a good rep with the EPA?"

"TBA, EPA, Jesus Christ, is everyone too stupid to just speak fucking English these days?"

"I don't think either of us would like the answer to that question, sir." Dothan was busy. He wanted Langhorne to get to the real point no matter how ugly. "What happened?"

"He told me that the studies needed to go ahead with the project could string out at least five years. That means nothing, no movement for at least six. None of our private interests are going to stick around for that long."

"They will if they believe they will ultimately see money."

"I'm not so sure."

"Here's the deal: I've talked to the TCEQ…"

"English, please."

"Texas Commission on Environmental Quality; what they tell me is that there is the possibility that the existing structures, as well as the prospected new developments, are in a five-hundred year flood plain. They are also concerned about the possibility of artifacts."

"Artifacts? What the hell are you talking about, JD?"

"There's the possibility that Native American artifacts could be buried in or around the area in question. They want to do an Archaeological Analysis."

"My God, how did we ever get running water or electricity in this country?"

"We wouldn't have. Not with the people who run things now a days."

Langhorne, perhaps because he felt the pangs of setback, was impressed by his son-in-law's command of the issue.

"What can we do?"

"Let them do their studies. It's better to not fight these things. They will win, and in the end, all that fighting them will do is cost *you* money, while simultaneously holding up the project."

"OK, I suppose you're right, JD—but this is ridiculous. A five hundred year flood plane! What the hell!"

"A Kawakawa arrowhead," Dothan added, referring to the archeological study.

"A Kawakawa arrowhead!" Langhorne followed. "I mean, aren't they the sad sons-of-bitches that smeared alligator blubber all over their naked bodies, wore tattoos and all kinds of savage shit?"

"I think you're right, sir. To ward off mosquitos, I think."

"I'd bet they wouldn't have outlawed DDT! Probably would have thought it was some sort of God or something!"

"Damn straight!"

The two laughed together.

Dothan was playing Langhorne, and Langhorne was eating it up. The good ol' boy talk was doing the trick. For years the representative had been intimidated by his caricature, Lyndon Johnson-like father-in-law. But something had happened to Dothan in the last few months, a transition had taken place. His confidence was growing with his knowledge. He now saw Langhorne as the redneck, Bubba, from *My Cousin Vinnie*; the guy who wanted to fight Joe Pesci to settle the two hundred dollars that he owed due to his losing at pool—the guy who always showed up at the most inopportune moment with an inadequate wad of bills, ready to settle. Dothan increasingly knew he would, at some point, have to deck Langhorne either metaphorically or literally. But now was the time to hang out.

"You're alright, JD," Langhorne declared after taking a sip of his single malt. "This is good stuff by the way."

"Single Barrel—18 years," Dothan replied, raising his glass in a toast."

"Say, on another subject, have you talked to my daughter lately? I've called her repeatedly and she hasn't returned any of my calls."

"Not lately. I think she's on some train trip through the Rockies or something."

"Jesus Christ, that woman is even more pampered and independent than her mother ever was; God rest her soul."

"Yes, sir."

The two decided to take their conversation over to the Austin Club on 9th and Congress.

∾

"God this place has changed!" Langhorne yelled to his walking companion so as to be audible above the rush hour traffic. The days were getting a little longer now and it was still light out. The air was crisp. Not a drop of sweat could be detected on either man.

"Yes it has changed. For the worse I think!"

"I agree, JD!"

Once inside the former opera house, the two made their way to the second floor. As they sat at the long bar, talking, the subject of Dothan's committee appointments inevitably arose.

"JD, I have to tell you, I'm really disappointed you didn't get on the Small Business Eco Development Committee like I asked you to. That could have worked wonders for us."

"It wasn't my decision sir, really. It's like all my chips were spent with the Special Joint Committee—a thing I didn't even ask for. Literally, the day I moved into my office Ron Martinez was there feeling me out."

"Strange. Speaking of the special committee, how is that state amnesty bill coming?"

"A guest worker bill, sir."

"What the hell's the difference?"

"This is how it breaks down: Although it is unconstitutional for an individual State from the Union to enter into an agreement—of any kind—with a foreign country, there is nothing to suggest that an individual State from the Union cannot enter into an agreement with an individual state of another country."

"Interesting."

"In this case we're talking about Mexico: the states of Coahuila and Nuevo Leon. We didn't come up with this ourselves, it's modeled from a law Utah passed a few years ago: the

Utah Compact. The Feds have as of yet to sue Utah over it. Of course we'll have to see what will happen now that the Amnesty Bill was passed and signed by the President."

"Well, we'll see how that goes. It's one thing to pass an unpopular law and have people lose health insurance, a whole other problem when you pass an unpopular law and children get blown to pieces!"

"And with more threats coming—from whom we don't know!"

"Amazing! Goddamn amazing! The Feds really are Goddamn idiots! Goddamn idiots!"

"Yes, it would appear that way. It really has struck at the heart of my liberalism. Maybe there are some things that states can administer better than Washington."

"Too many people—it's too big, the country is too big, JD. It's not about an ideology, hell I'm Pro-Choice, but to hell with gay marriage!"

"I know, sir, you've expressed your disgust with that notion to me on numerous occasions."

"That issue aside, the federal government has really screwed things up. I mean, do you realize how many people casually talk about secession? And not the fringe-types, I mean respectable professionals of different backgrounds. It's becoming mainstream, JD. And that Reed Jackson character, if he keeps it up, he'll be more popular than Davy Crockett!"

"Is that right...sir?" Dothan had not really heard Langhorne; for just as the words left his 40 proof lips, he witnessed Rachael Logan enter the room. She was not alone.

"…are you listening to me, JD? Goddamnit, you're just like Jessica, always drifting off. What is it with your generation—hello?"

"I'm sorry sir, I agree with you."

"Agree with what? I didn't express an opinion."

"How out of the ordinary…will you excuse me…? I have to piss." Dothan lifted his butt from the bar stool and headed towards the bathroom located at the back of the dining area, where Rachael and her party had just entered.

The lady senator had not detected him as he meandered past the long buffet line, where she now stood. The man she had entered with was obviously her husband. When he crossed back from the restroom, he observed that an elderly woman and two children now joined the two: a boy and girl.

Should I introduce myself? he wondered.

He stood between two miscellaneous tables, spying over at Langhorne. His father-in-law fidgeted on his stool, obviously impatient. He decided no on the introductions. But before he could make his escape back to the bar, Rachael spotted him.

Dothan felt strange after meeting Rachael's family. Her husband, Donald, was a nice enough fellow, but a total square. Plus, he was balding badly. Throwing back his full mane of gothic locks as he strutted back towards the bar, he could not help but feel superior to the man.

Her children are attractive, he thought, *and very well behaved*. The old woman reminded him of his own mother. For an instant he was reminded of a chronic pang. *A nice family he surmised*, without a suggestion of envy.

II.

"I've tried calling the number I have for Warren Jenkins and it's disconnected. It must have been a cellphone, because he always answered it in the field," Tryphena informed Dothan as they marched towards the weekly Special Joint Committee meeting.

"What made you feel you needed to follow up on that?" he asked.

"Woman's intuition."

"I'll ask Chairman Jackson about it. Not that there is anything to know. Consultants are mercenaries."

"Perhaps. But ask about it anyway, JD."

"I'm going to, like I already said."

The meeting had already started when Dothan entered.

"Let the record show that Representative Dothan is now present—mark the time," Chairman Jackson said, instructing the clerk without looking at the tardy party in question. Reed had been in mid-speech when Dothan entered. He continued, "I find it disturbing that we're having so many problems on the House side with our bill. Representative Martinez, what do think is the problem? It should already be waiting on the Calendar Committee to release."

"Chairman, I can assure you that I'm doing everything I can at this point. Have you considered that your recent comments in McAllen might have something to do with the present trepidation?"

"No, I just think that the committee members might not have been stimulated properly."

"What do you mean?" another committee member asked.

"I mean sir, that what we need to do is start constituent calls in mass. The public overwhelmingly supports my comments. The voters finally feel they have a voice. All the polls show this. Let's get staff off of their butts and get them to contact the respective House committee members, as well. A few more targeted press releases might be in order, too."

"You hear that JD? We might need you and Senator Logan to pick up your PR," Martinez added.

"Where is Rachael?" Dothan asked. He could immediately tell Reed had taken offense at this breech of formality.

"Senator Logan's family is in town. She was unable to make it this evening. I will brief her myself later."

Discussion ensued about the merits and difficulties surrounding the legislation. When the hour had perished, the group adjourned. Dothan approached the Chairman. "Do you mind if I have a moment of your time, Chairman?"

"Certainly. What is it, sir?"

"Nothing really, I was just curious; it's my understanding that you know Warren Jenkins and Jack Clark."

"Who?"

Dothan repeated himself, and then added, "The two were my campaign team."

"Ah, yes, perhaps I do. I've worked with so many different campaign-types through the years that sometimes I forget specific names—particularly from long ago."

"But according to your Campaign Finance Report, they were in your employment just this past election cycle."

"Can I ask what exactly this concerns, Representative Dothan?"

"Nothing, I was just inquiring about a mutual business associate."

"So you've inquired. Will that be all?"

"Yes, sir."

Later, back at his office, Dothan discussed his questioning of Reed with Tryphena. "There is something wrong with that guy, he's fucking creepy."

"Yeah he is. You're just figuring that out?"

"I've always thought he was a pompous, elite asshole. But those are a dime-a-dozen up here. But there is just something not right about him."

"Your female intuition?" Tryphena jested.

"Whatever it is, try to find out how to get in touch with Jenkins. He's running a business, there has to be a way to contact him."

Dothan stayed late at the Capitol going over bills. When he finally gathered his things and left his office it was after midnight. The halls were empty. Listening to the metronome of his own footsteps the man became hypnotized by his own presence. Hubris was gripping him. Musing on the day's events he gloated to himself on how he had tamed Langhorne. *His corporate welfare will have to wait.* And Rachael's family? *I missed out on nothing.*

As he exited the elevator at the parking garage, Dothan felt almost satisfied with his existence.

This could not last.

chapter Thirteen

Dothan was sinking. The previous week absorbed with work had depleted him. The barriers his mind had constructed so as to exile his heart, had come crashing down. The compartments that he had plotted so meticulously were filling with emotion, one by one. This intricate building up and tearing down was accomplished in a matter of days.

Listening to Gordon Lightfoot's "Sundown," Dothan hummed to himself, sitting on his back patio. The numerous empty beer cans and pile of cigarette butts littered around his chair gave testimony to the sentiments above; so well expressed by the Canadian. A great contradiction lived inside Dothan, although he had such hope for the world, regarding himself he was fatalistic.

This found expression in art.

Although given to brooding, Dothan, being a creature of action, acted. Words began to order themselves, and in rapid succession. From the patio to the den he had already forgotten several "perfect" lines. No bother, when it flowed, it flowed. If the compartments were filling with emotion, his pen acted as anchor.

It took little polishing the next morning, as he sat in his office typing it up. As he now looked at what he had accomplished, he felt better about his resting at the bottom of the abyss. It had been a long time since he had sculpted language that he thought captured the inspiration. The man had begun to doubt if he had any real poetry left in him at all. Now, at least with regards to his own regard, he still did.

Once printed, he stuffed the single page in a hand-addressed envelope; Tryphena was asked to deliver it.

Her errand afforded her time for reflection: *What's he doing now, addressing a letter to 'Rachael'? He's been acting strange all morning. He is so inconsistent. 'Programed to self-destruct' is what it says on the bottom of one of his feet—I guarantee it. God stamped it on there at birth. But why would God do that to a guy like JD? For all his flaws he is, at his core, a good man…I think. What am I thinking? I don't really believe in all that nonsense. Or do I really? He is his own master, either way. He has privilege.*

Tryphena made the delivery and returned to the Capitol Extension. The rest of the day she was displaced by a mood of unwanted sagacity broken only by silent anger.

❧

For days, Dothan sauntered through his routine: long hours on the floor, Recreation and Culture Committee hearings, etc. Another Special Joint Committee on Immigration Reform meeting went past and no sign or word from Rachael. Dothan was a man of experience, and thus he understood that even passion must be calculated. He resisted the undertow that insisted he confront her. His resistance was getting weaker by the moment. For Dothan, waiting for Rachael's response was like one afflicted with a terrible ailment, waiting to get in to see a physician.

Rachael had been away. Upon returning from her district, where she had been celebrating her son's birthday, she found the envelope in question.

Rachael Logan was a classical woman. Her sensibility (what vulgarians would mistake as elitist) was authentically attracted to the graceful things of life. As a girl growing up in Austin, when all her girlfriends were enthralled with the likes of Brooke Shields and Madonna, she was obsessed with Princess Grace; this generational oddity occurring after watching *To Catch a Thief* on cable TV. Her attraction to John David, which on the surface could appear a case of 'opposites attract,' was in truth quite the opposite. While most modern women would be, at best, perplexed by the presentation of a sonnet and at worst disgusted. A thing like a poem, which appealed to both her femininity and her independence, for Rachael was an aphrodisiac.

She was a girl and I was a
 fool.
She was flippant and free—and I didn't know,
The nature of what glued the world
 together:

The gristle'd seams where nothing green can grow.

She was a girl and I was a
> *child.*

Both as righteous as a rain muscled creek,
That swept us along faster than we
> *knew:*

Months like years, days as long as summer weeks.
She was a girl and I was a
> *wound—*

She realized finally she'd never
> *heal—*
In crowned Womanhood like an Easter morn
She rose from youth with the ease of a
> *wheel.*

She was a girl and I was a fool –
And long since grown up, as I have grown cruel.

In an age of ugliness, animalism and the lowest of lowest common denominators, John David Dothan exhibited that rarest of traits: humanity. Having spent a decade in the company of stiff Republicans, she had forgotten what artistic expression looked and sounded like. Dothan had summoned a powerful undertow, indeed.

Marriage, for too many, becomes a laborious habit. It is usually hinged upon things removed from it: children, finances, etc. But that notion is based upon the premise that marriage is a compact rooted in individual fulfillment. In fact, it is rooted in the things that are removed from fulfillment. It is a responsibility. Civilization without marriage is quite possibly impossible. Dothan often pondered the possibility that we may all be, in fact, slaves to civilization.

Rachael Logan had long been unhappy in her marriage. There were a myriad of reasons for this. She often thought, oddly, that their adopted children had caused this rift. The maternal instinct is selfless, and can find expression in many ways. Paternalism is selfish, and rarely accepts, ultimately, that which is not blood. Rachael and her husband had been drifting apart for many years. Whether he was a good man or a bad man was of no consequence; time had changed things for the worse. Rachael had become bored with her habit. She was ready to be taken out to sea. But the prospect of drowning…?

Rachael Logan had a choice to make. Her decision had the potential to spawn unintended consequences. Sitting at her desk, dwelling on the blank parchment, textured letterhead, the ballpoint hovering just above the surface, she felt like an ancient queen leveling an edict, an edict that could have repercussions on innocent lives. As she scribed her reply to Dothan, this fact she understood above all others.

A staffer was sent to dispatch the correspondence. Pam was on the receiving end. She left the unopened letter from Senator Logan's office on Dothan's desk. Returning late from yet another grueling day on the floor, Dothan tore open the letter like it was Christmas morning.

Dear John David,

You have won. I surrender. I am not convinced that you are not the devil himself. If so, then that would explain the silver tongue. You bastard, why are you doing this to me? Is my unhappiness with my own life that obvious; or, is it your unhappiness? I would like to believe that it is because you never stopped loving me. That somehow, for a quarter century, you carried a flame. It was my belief, after discovering that you had won your race, that I could treat you as nothing more than a colleague. But then, when session started, and you were here under the same roof as I, I knew that I would find difficulty with that. That is why I did not come to see you. Still, things arranged themselves as they did – for a reason? I used to believe that all things happened for a reason. That life worked itself out. I don't know anymore.

Remember the cabin in Dripping Springs? It's still there. Alicia's folk's still own it and I am still good friends with her. What are you doing this Thursday night? Will you meet me there? I have left the address at the bottom of this letter. Google it or GPS (I know your truck doesn't have GPS.) Find it John David.

You have won. I surrender.

By the way, your poem was beautiful. Though, I have to say, you are wrong about the 'ease of a wheel' part. That's your narcissism speaking. You always had a penchant for self-pity.
Love, Rachael.

A swelling took place in Dothan's face, a swelling of emotion. Tears began, which he could not control. It would be an overstatement to say he wept, but in so as much as the cowboy was capable, he did.

Twenty-five years is a long, long time. No one in the world knew what he had harbored. In many ways he had for himself, as Benet had so eloquently commented on General Lee, '*kept his heart a secret to the end, safe from all the picklocks of biographers.*' Life had crushed him. But he wore his defeat quite well—for after all, he did have art. The scars looked good on him. But they were still scars. Scars that refused to surrender their story, until now. It would be an exaggeration to say the flame burned unwaveringly. It was more like an ache, something that recurs with a change in the barometric pressure: an old broken bone. But it was there. It was definitely there. And neither the cynics nor the businessmen could ever confiscate it from his possession. And now…? Now he had his chance to consummate the past.

Just below Rachael's signature he scribed a large, '*YES.*'

The letter was to be dispatched back to the Lady Senator's office. But before Pam could administer the function, Tryphena returned to the office. Inquiring as to what the staff had been doing, she was informed of the information volley between Logan and Dothan. She made sure to deliver the letter herself.

The more reckless Dothan was acting the more paranoid she became: *I wish I could sit down with this woman. Who is she anyway? Someone he once knew? She is so proper I'm sure she's a snot; probably never had to worry about paying a bill in her life. Just like Jessica. I'm sure he never looked longingly at a working girl a day in his life. I just hope she knows what she's doing because it's obvious that he hasn't a clue. 'Rose of your Memory' for him maybe, but the thorn is stuck in my ass.*

Thursday night was just forty-eight hours from now. For Dothan it seemed like an eternity. Although the days were long at the Capitol, he spent his mornings and nights trying to better his appearance. Hitting the gym, which he had neglected since session started, he furiously worked out. His caloric intake had been largely beer, of late, so this presented a problem with his midsection. His regimen was so intense that afterward it hurt to go to the bathroom. At home he experimented with a teeth-whitening kit because he could not find a dentist who could see him that quickly. This was futile, as he could not resist from smoking during the necessary time allotted for whitening.

In his few spare instances, Dothan expected Rachael to change her mind.

Rachael had no intention of changing her mind. If anything, she now, for reasons long directly associated with Dothan, considered herself a fallen woman. It was the only true thread that ran through her life. If she were a puppet, the strings were attached to John David. But she was not a puppet; she was an individual and responsible for her own actions.

Why can't I resist this undertow? she asked herself.

Rachael was an intellectual woman. She had read everything from *Romanticism and Consciousness* to the *Feminine Mystique*; the bulk of her reading, independent of college curriculum, like Dothan, possessed that rarest of ethos: a passion for knowledge for the sake of knowledge. This was most un-American of them both. Her conservatism, though perhaps rooted in a regional bias, was to be found in a personal tragedy.

Rachael considered herself a fallen woman….Absolutely.

chapter Fourteen

Harry Spencer, like too many politicians, was a megalomaniacal narcissist. This flaw is what had enabled his decadent lifestyle, however ill-advised given his political career. His defeat at the hands of Dothan and his team continued to eat at him like a malignance. Now, his life torn asunder by the nastiness of the campaign, he was determined to exact revenge. He had no idea how, only that he must.

His first rule of order was to begin researching those that had brought him down. He wasn't entirely without resources. The squalid apartment was necessary to create the illusion that he had been wiped out in the divorce. What was not on record, however, was the seventy thousand cold hard dollars he had accumulated in a safety deposit box over so many years.

Harry's sense of entitlement regarding his own position as a state representative limited his sense of urgency during the campaign. By the time he had discovered that he was being out-maneuvered by his opponent, it was too late. He had learned from this mistake.

He hired a private detective and the PI set about delving into every aspect of John David Dothan's life. Little of real interest revealed itself, at least with regards to the controversial. One interesting fact was uncovered, however, and that being his relationship to Rachael Logan. Apparently the two had graduated from Stephen F. Austin High School in Austin, Texas; and in the same year. But did they know each other?

After hunting down several graduates from their specific class it was reported that the two had dated. There was even one report of a possible pregnancy. Although this was simply hearsay, it could put into question the virtue of the Right's family values cover girl.

But there were far more ominous issues that would soon reveal themselves.

Delving deep into Dothan's Campaign Finance Reports, the private investigator was led in a myriad of directions.

Harry Spencer was at a convenience store pumping gas and watching several teenage girls walk into the respective establishment, ogling their bare thighs glistening in the supple air, when the inconvenience of a call occurred. Recognizing the number, he answered his cell. "Yes Stern, what is it?"

"Mr. Spencer, are you busy? Can you talk?" Rusty Stern, the easy going, former state trooper from Montgomery, Alabama asked, sensing his client's agitation.

"I'm talking. What is it?"

"Well sir, you say you've been friends with Reed Jackson for some time?"

"Since '68. We served side-by-side—stationed in Na Trang. Why?"

"Harry, I've found some things—disturbing things, I think—that if they mean anything at all…well…"

"What the fuck are you talking about Stern?" Harry interrupted.

"Well sir…after pouring over these Campaign Finance Reports, I've come across something disturbing."

"You've said that! Cut to the chase!" Harry ordered, replacing the gas pump.

"OK, too hell with it…I'll just say it: I think that Reed Jackson financed your opponent—at least initially."

"Stern, are you drunk?"

"Not yet."

"So you're serious?"

"Dead serious, sir."

"How in the hell did you come up with that?"

"Quite simply by reading the filed reports."

"I get that. Explain!" Harry hollered as he started his Range Rover.

"Warren Jenkins and Jack Clark were Dothan's campaign team…"

"I know that. So what?"

"Well, Dothan hired Jenkins and Clark Inc. That's what shows up on *his* report. On Reed Jackson's report, for that same filing period, there is a payment to 'Victory Ballot.'"

"So what. What does that mean?"

"Victory Ballot is Warren Jenkins! It's just another name he conducts business under. Most of these consultants use several entities. It is how they work incognito."

"So what does that prove?" Maybe it was for something else, some other campaign."

"That's a possibility. I'm going to comb through all the other reports for that period—every state rep. and state senators' race, at least."

"Jesus Christ, how long will that take?"

"A few days—I'm already halfway done. So far Dothan was their only client."

"Why would Reed do something like this? It doesn't make sense. I was part of the plan."

"The plan, sir?"

"Nothing. Never mind. Call me when you have an answer."

"Will do, sir."

Harry Spencer was confused and on the brink of devastation. His mind reeled back and forth—a tug of war between what his gut told him might be real and how he wanted things to be. Yes, Harry had known Reed Jackson for some forty-five years; owed his political career to him. It was Reed who talked him into running all those years ago. But it went back further, back to the Vietnam War. What an awful time that was.

He pulled the black Range Rover out onto the highway and thought back on those ancient days. Now, divorced from his wife, his law practice nearly evaporated, with no children, Reed was the only link to times gone by...

~

Da Nang Air Base was just 85 miles south of the De-militarized zone; the 17th parallel; the border between North and South. By 1968, it was witnessing upwards of seventy thousand takeoffs and landings per month.

Warrant Officer Harry Spencer served in the First Cavalry Division, or Airmobile, when First Lieutenant Reed Jackson arrived at Da Nang. Lieutenant Reed, having lead and survived several ground missions into the jungle, was well respected. Although brash and often a bully, his men were loyal to him as he continuously brought them back alive. Reed Jackson credited his success (if it could be called success, as there were no clear victories), on his unwavering faith in Jesus Christ. Few were prepared to argue the point.

He had, however, been wounded recently. Initially a flesh wound where a bullet had passed through his shoulder, the area had grown infected. He was placed on leave and rather than indulge in a little R&R, Reed decided to participate in a Christian-based program to aid his fellow soldiers hurt both physically and mentally by their experiences in combat.

While briefly serving in Saigon, Harry Spencer had become addicted to whoring and heroin. And while whoring took time, heroin, readily available, required only a few seconds. But it was a grisly convenience. It wasn't long before he fell severely ill with hepatitis.

It took several weeks before Harry was discharged. Although weak from withdrawal, the liver was healthy enough for some activity. The activity prescribed was spiritual cleansing. That is how Warrant Officer Harry Spencer met Lieutenant Reed

Jackson. The chemistry just worked. Harry was a couple of years older than Reed, but Reed was the ranking officer. A balance was struck.

Harry Spencer, once a nihilistic rowdy Texan, was 'born again' under the care of Arlington, Virginia native, Reed Jackson…

~

Harry Spencer was confused and on the brink of devastation.

A couple of days passed with no word from Stern. Harry had forsaken all vices with the exception of those associated with the flesh, because without those, he was as restless as a rodent in a cage. He tried smoking, eating and drinking, but those activities could not simulate freedom. Only masturbation gave relief. At his age, this required much time. Nothing but a verdict on Reed's status as a traitor could open the gates of the hell that he was currently living in.

At last he called.

"Well, it's official." Stern said, regretfully.

"Define 'official.'"

"I've looked over everything. Warren Jenkins has worked with a lot of candidates through the years, worked for Reed on numerous occasions…but nothing else corresponds with our particular time frame. Nothing. It had to be on behalf of Dothan. I can't see that it could be for any other reason. He fucked you Harry, plain and simple."

Harry sat frozen. There was a protracted silence.

"Sir, are you still there…hello?"

"I'm still here. I've never been much of an ethics report kind of guy, Stern. But I understand that this bullshit is all public record."

"Yes, yes it is."

"So why would Reed conceivably do this out in the open?"

"Classic move: You do things in the light of day and no one suspects anything, and no questions are asked. Pull the moving van up in broad daylight and clean out the house while the family is at work and school. That's much smarter than kicking down the door in the middle of the night. Reed's a crook, Harry."

"And there is no honor among thieves."

"What does that mean?"

"Oh nothing, nothing at all Stern. There is a certain freedom to knowing, as there is a certain freedom in knowing you are alone."

"I'm sorry, Harry. I know this has to be hard to take, with your divorce and all."

"And all…most definitely, Stern."

"Is there anything else I can help you with, sir?"

"Perhaps posthumously."

"Excuse me?"

"We will have to see Stern. Send in your latest invoice, I know I've had to have eaten through the retainer by now."

Harry Spencer was no longer confused, but he was still on the brink of devastation. *What should I* do? he contemplated. *Should I confront Reed?* He wished desperately to do so.

So he did.

Spencer sat in the vacant parking lot of an out of the way, defunct movie rental store, smoking a cigarette and sipping a Bacardi and Coke. He took out his cell phone and called his old military buddy of 45 years. Reed answered, first try.

"Reed, this is Harry."

"Yes Harry, how are you?"

"Not well…Reed…not well."

"What's the matter? Is there something I can do?"

Harry was having difficulty speaking, his emotions had seized his tongue just like they had when he tried to convince his wife not to leave him.

"Harry, are you still there?" Reed asked forcibly.

"Why Reed?" Harry's voice was trembling. It was obvious that he was choking up.

"Why what, Harry? What on earth are you talking about?"

"Was it that I'm sick? You could've asked me not to run again if you thought I was a liability. I would've stepped down. Why Dothan, that unemployed guitar player?"

"What are you talking about? Dothan?"

"You know what I'm talking about Reed." Harry was getting control of himself, "You hired Warren Jenkins and that fucking Jack Clark to assassinate me! You fucking traitor!" Harry screamed.

"Harry, you are obviously having a breakdown. Where are you? I'll come and get you, take you to get help."

"Why, so you can do to me literally what you personally did to my livelihood? I know what you did Reed. I know! And now I'm going to blow it all open—all of it!"

"Harry, you are obviously having a breakdown. Let me help you."

"You burn in hell Reed Jackson! You will burn in hell!"

"Harry? Harry?" Reed pleaded into the phone, but Harry had already hung up.

Reed sat regretful but unperturbed. He dialed Martinez.

"What is it Reed?" Martinez asked, concerned, as it was late.

"Harry knows about Dothan."

"Oh my God! What should we do?"

"Please don't panic. We should now do what we should have done already."

~

Harry returned to his lonely apartment with a bag of Chinese food and several adult DVDs. He sat at his desk, the only piece of nice furniture in the place. He took out three sheets of old House of Representatives stationary and began to hand write three letters; all of an identical message.

chapter Fifteen

Dothan sat in his office deep in thought. His concentration was interrupted by the patter of rain on the skylights that arched just outside his window. He rose from his big brown leather chair and pulled the blinds open with his fingers and peered up into the dismal March day. The raindrops on the slanted rectangular glass created shadows on the wall and floor of the extension atrium, which looked like amoebas under a microscope.

Thursday had arrived.

The Senate had already adjourned until next Monday, but the House was still bustling. Dothan had withdrawn himself from the floor by using the excuse that he had business in his district. But he wasn't going south; he was going west. Earlier Rachael had texted a simple, 'Tonight?' to his cell phone. He had replied with a simple, 'Yes.'

The staff was oblivious, except Tryphena, who sensed something strange. *He's acting weird again. District business...*

what business? He hasn't said anything to me about this…nothing. I just hope he doesn't have 'Programed to self-destruct' tattooed on his dick! Should I just go in there and ask him if something is going on, and if so, what it is?

It was past five and Tryphena decided to cut the staff loose until Monday. The rumor up and down the halls was that the speaker was giving everyone Friday off. This was unusual, and Pam resisted. Tryphena had to nearly push her out the door.

Dothan was standing motionless at the window when Tryphena crossed the threshold to his office. Her tongue and lips moved to shape the sounds that would get to the bottom of his odd demeanor this afternoon, but before any noise could be made, the phone rang. She vacated his office undetected by Dothan and answered the call.

"Yeah sugar, is my husband there?" Tryphena's greeting received.

"Ms. Dothan?"

"Does he have another wife? What are we, Mormons? Yes, this is Jessica."

As usual, the woman made little sense. Tryphena always felt a sense of panic when Jessica called. Jessica rarely called, which further justified her fear. Panic usurped instinct and she answered in the affirmative. With the phone on hold she again entered Dothan's office. While he still stood by the window, he turned towards the door when she crossed the threshold. He shook his head in an emphatic 'NO!'

"The phone is on hold, JD, she can't hear us? I've already told her you were here!"

"Well tell her you were mistaken!" Dothan demanded, and then turned back towards the window.

Frustrated, Tryphena grabbed wads of her taut black hair. *I'm going to rip it all out any minute!* After taking a deep breath… she picked up the receiver. "Ms. Dothan?"

"You don't sound like JD."

"No, ma'am," Tryphena laughed nervously, "I was mistaken, I thought he had returned to the office, but looking up at the TV I can see that they are still on the floor."

"Still on the floor? God, why would anyone want that job? It pays peanuts and you work all the time."

"Yes, ma'am."

"Well, tell him I called."

Tryphena had just barely hung up the phone when Dothan blew past her. He was halfway down the hall before she could stick her head out of the office to remind him, "Remember to call your wife!" she shouted with a degree of worry and consternation.

Dothan wasted no time getting out of the Capitol Complex. He did not stop and talk to the garage caretaker, as he was wont to do. He did not remove his tie before setting off. Getting out of the Capitol Complex was one thing, but getting out of Austin was another. Resigning himself that he would be stuck in traffic, he stopped and filled up the old truck and grabbed a six-pack and some smokes. He was more excited than nervous. To ease his nerves he threw in English Beat, popped a brew, and lit a smoke.

～

Rachael had arrived to the cabin earlier that afternoon; she was more nervous than excited.

Alicia had warned her that the cabin wasn't in the best of shape. It was rarely visited and hadn't been cleaned to any degree in several years. The place had its share of cobwebs and dust.

She slipped out of her suit and into a pair of jeans and a work shirt and proceeded to bust out the cleaning supplies. With Enya's *Watermark* lilting on the stereo, Rachael gave the old place the proverbial once over twice. Her mind raced from thought to thought. She knew that John David was expecting to make love; she wasn't so sold on the idea and hoped she might resist. She was more interested in the reunion aspect of it all. Life rarely afforded one the anomaly of a rewind. But here she was, sweeping and dusting off the spot where arguably, she and the love of her life had first lain together.

Occasionally, the notion of her husband and children would invade her mind. Although she might cringe for an instant here and there, and while the millstone of her entire belief system was cracked thoroughly, she did not mind that the entryway to her life could, at any moment, come down upon her and those she cared for. Life had already crushed Rachael Logan, in its own silent way. Alternating between maid and chef, she continuously played the CD. She wished to leave it on indefinitely, but worried that John David would think it not edgy enough.

John David had texted her regarding the traffic he was sitting in upon his departure, so Rachael assumed she had over an hour to get ready. Her phone was kept on her person at all times so as not to miss the angry call from John David informing her he was lost. She had a lovely red dress she planned on wearing. But all of these contrivances were shot when the chug of the '74 Ford announced itself over the hill!

What should I do?

Suddenly, there was a knock at the door. She had no other choice but to open it. There in the fading light of day, stood the dark figure of a well-tailored man; while she, having engaged in cleaning and cooking stood in soiled shirt and jeans while her pulled back hair fell about her face.

John David stared at her greedily.

She attempted to wave the bothersome strands from her face, but accustomed to high heels, in this shortened state, she felt intimidated.

"Can I come in?" Dothan asked, placing his boot across the threshold.

"Of course…you're early John David…I had plans…," she girlishly pleaded, gently hitting her fists on his chest in protest.

John David set his bag down and with the reach of his hand, moved the thick band of brown hair from Rachael's glistening face. "You are the most beautiful thing I have ever seen." He spoke in the lowest register of his baritone voice. With that, he quickly grabbed her by the waist and hoisted her up in his arms. "Where is the goddamned bedroom?" he demanded as he swung her around the cabin kitchen.

"Would you put me down, sir?" she retorted, half playfully, half genuinely startled.

"Sir? Are you sure you are talking to a gentleman, my lady?" Dothan found the bedroom, it did not appear to be the room from a quarter century ago, but he did not care. He threw her down on the ancient creaking bed and proceeded to fuck Rachael into intense absolute orgasm.

For a few minutes afterward the two lay wordless, panting, sporadically clothed and with sweat gushing from their skin.

"It's hot in here," Dothan stated stoically.

"I know. All they have are window units."

"You didn't switch any on?"

"No, it was cold when I got here…I got to cleaning and cooking and…"

The music from the stereo suddenly became audible to Dothan. "What the fuck are we listening to?" he interrupted.

"Enya—I knew you'd hate it."

"I don't hate it…I don't hate it at all. I *love* Enya."

"Really? Rachael asked, surprised. She turned on her side and placed her arm across John David's dampened chest; her naked leg draped his thigh like a storm-collapsed sail across a flooding stern. Slowly she tugged on his saturated stomach hair with her thumb and index finger. "You don't have any cigarettes do you?"

"I have a carton behind the seat of my truck. Since when do you smoke?"

"Since I became an adulteress."

"What are we living in, biblical times? We're not going to start feeling guilty now, are we?"

"Don't say things like that John David…please. Don't ruin this for me."

"Hey, I was just kidding. I'm sorry. I didn't mean anything

by it," he responded, realizing that he had somehow hurt her, though oblivious as to why.

"It's OK," Rachael replied with an air of resignation; like one on a raft headed for exile, looking back at her native shore.

Dothan was the first to get up from bed. He hopped off the mattress, stripped completely naked and began changing his clothes. Rachael also stripped naked, was not going to let John David's cowboy-like entry spoil her need for romance. She went to the bathroom to shower.

It was late March and with sun now set, it was getting cool. Decked out in a western shirt, cowboy boots and jeans, Dothan, armed with a flashlight, surveyed the nearby land-scape, looking for firewood. He was conscious of snakes that may have recently awakened. When he returned to the cabin, he discovered an entirely made over Rachael.

The cabin's electric lights had been almost completely turned off. An array of candles littered the place; softly illuminating the natural soft browns and grays of the rustic lodging. This was the second time John David Dothan had ever visited this particular smudge on the Earth. The first time, the flippant eye of youth had failed to really absorb the surroundings. For a quarter century, this spot had been an afterimage. Now, sitting at this small rectangular table of rough red oak, a beautiful creature dressed in a red dress sitting opposite him, the smell of some rich Italian sauce simmering on the stove, two glasses of Merlot poured; now it revealed itself to him. The walls were littered with ancient photographs and faded Texana; a menagerie of branding irons near the fireplace; the subtle scent of wood and leather. This was the 'blood's country' that McMurtry had tried to capture in his early novels. Yes, this home, this place, indeed this land, which he had so disregarded for so long—up until this instant; this was the actual remnants of a family enterprise that reached back more than a century. He took comfort in knowing there was always something larger than one's self. It helped to temporarily mask his ever-present feelings of failure.

"I think I'm a little underdressed," he stated matter-of-factly.

"It's OK, I don't mind. If you mind, there is always your suit…I hung it up in one of the closets."

"If you don't mind I'd rather not. And thank you, I could have done that myself."

"I don't mind. Perhaps I'm the one who's overdressed."

"What I said when I arrived…I wasn't lying. You are the most beautiful woman I have ever seen."

"I think…actually…you called me a 'thing.' 'The most beautiful *thing* I have ever seen.' I believe that is how you phrased it."

Dothan sat a bit confused, not knowing how to reply to her sudden jesting. "Whatever I said, apparently worked."

"Apparently."

"A toast," John David abruptly declared, lifting his glass, "a toast to the present."

"The present…not the past?"

"The past as well!"

"But not the future?"

"The future?"

~

The two enjoyed the delicious chicken Parmesan Rachael had prepared. It was one of John David's favorite dishes. Dothan switched quickly back to beer, killing them—as Rachael saw it—at an alarmingly fast rate.

"You better slow down there!"

"What? You sound like my wife. I can handle it. It's just beer."

"Sounds like famous last words to me. That can't be good for your high blood pressure— that and those cigarettes."

"So she says after bumming one…and…how much have you had to drink?" he countered, lifting the bottle of Merlot. "And how do you know about my blood pressure? I don't remember ever telling you about that."

"I found your prescription; it must have fallen out of your bag. You should be more responsible with that."

"I can handle it."

"Yes, so you keep saying." There was a protracted silence. Rachael finished chewing a piece of meat. "What about your wife? You never talk about her…ever. I don't think you have ever mentioned her come to think of it."

"You've never asked about her, come to think of it."

"You don't need to get snarky John David, I'm just asking."

"Well, there's not much to tell, really…Jessica is just Jessica."

"Wow, that's descriptive—and from a poet no less."

"What do you want me to say: that she is a self-absorbed, self-regarding bitch?"

"Where did that come from?

"I'm sorry. Um…Jessica is just Jessica."

"OK."

"What about your husband. I met him and he seems like a nice fella. A little thin up top, but a nice fella."

"That wasn't called for John David. He can't help that he's losing his hair. It may happen to you at some point, you know."

"I'm kidding. So, tell me about him."

"The one word that I would use to describe Donald is 'detached.'"

"Sounds like my wife."

"Ah, now we're getting somewhere."

"You lay out the adjectives and adverbs and I'll check the appropriate boxes."

"Anyway, as I was saying, it's like he's been emotionally MIA for at least half of our marriage."

"Check!" he exclaimed, getting up from the table.

"I'm being serious John David."

"I am too," he said, reaching into the fridge for another beer.

"I know he loves Matthew and Kathryn, but as they get older he just seems…he just seems…"

"Detached?" Dothan asked facetiously, returning to his chair; wanting to avoid discussion of children.

"Yes, detached." Rachael removed the paper napkin from her lap, and with her elbows on the table, she folded her hands together. She continued, "I wouldn't be surprised if he's had or is having an affair."

"Really? You're still wearing your ring, I see," John David observed.

"You're just realizing that? A habit I suppose. What about yours, you don't wear it anymore?"

"I lost it a long time ago."

"Donald has lost several rings. I always insist he get a new one."

"I lost it a long time ago."

With lovemaking and dinner out of the way, the two wished to nestle down on the couch together. Rachael changed in the bathroom as John David rummaged through a bin of old DVDs and VHS tapes, looking for anything interesting to watch. He faintly heard something outside.

"Do you hear that?" he asked Rachael as she emerged from the bathroom.

"Hear what?" she asked, disappointed.

"It sounds like a kitten meowing. Listen."

"What? Where?"

The two moved towards the window to inspect, but the glare on the glass and the blackness outside made the source of the sound impossible to determine.

"Did Alicia say anything about a cat?" John David asked.

"No. They don't have a cat up here. Who would take care of it?"

"I don't know, maybe it's a barn cat, eats mice and armadillos and what not."

"Cats don't eat armadillos, dummy."

"Who you calling dummy?" he asked playfully, closing the curtains. Now, to Rachael's relief, he finally noticed her. "Look at you…you look so beautiful." Rachael was dressed in a large flannel that covered her panties; her naked olive legs showing; her brown hair clipped up in a chip clip.

"To the past?" she said, innocently.

John David could not resist; he forced her into his arms and the two infidels began kissing intensely. The cry of the alleged kitten sounded again. "Listen, it sounds so tiny. It has to be a kitten," she interrupted.

"We should try and feed him." The two were now talking in nearly a whisper.

"With what?" I doubt they have any pet food, and if they did it would be stale to boot."

"It's a stray wilderness cat, I doubt he'd mind. What about the chicken? Is there anything left over from dinner?"

"I have some left over from my plate, but it has spiced breading and sauce all over it. I don't want to hurt its tummy."

"Hurt its tummy? It's been living out here on mice and armadillos. What are you talking about, hurting its tummy?"

"Cats don't eat armadillos," Rachael insisted in a muted tone. She went to the kitchen and scraped the chicken scraps onto a paper plate. The paper plate was placed just outside the backdoor. A light was left on so the two could periodically spy from the window.

~

A fire snapped passively from the stove, warming the quaint den. Rachael and John David were currently settled into the sofa watching an old Gregory Peck film called *Beloved Infidels*: a true story about F. Scott Fitzgerald and his mistress. Fidgeting was an issue, and eventually they settled on

Rachael sitting up with John David's head in her lap; the lady senator ran her fingers through the freshman representative's hair. But the smell of Rachael's naked thighs was too much for John David. It wasn't long before his libido took over. The two were most likely too tired for sex—again, but kissing ensued and continued into the bedroom.

Rachael awoke several hours later, needing to pee. John David lay crashed and snoring. The fire had extinguished itself and the cabin was cold. After relieving herself, she trotted carefully to the window near the backdoor. The food had vanished. Returning to bed she hoped it was the alleged kitten who had partaken and not a mouse or armadillo.

~

John David's eyes grudgingly cracked open. The morning had by now filled the room. This reluctance to face a new day was immediately doused when a pair of soft lips met his rough-hewn cheek.

"Good morning sleepy head!" Rachael said, jumping out of bed. "Burr, it's freezing in here, John David!" she said, shivering.

"Not in here. Come back to bed. What time is it?"

"After nine! Are you on the floor today?"

"I have no idea."

"You might want to find out. We're adjourned until Monday. I'm going to make some coffee," she added, pacing quickly out of the room due to the cold.

"Of course you're off until Monday—you're the Senate, we're just the House!" he shouted back, sarcastically.

Following a few cups of coffee and a visit to the john, John David was ready for bed. Rachael was having none of it. "I have to get going. I have some business appointments in District later today. I do have a law practice to maintain. They don't pay us in the Senate any more than they pay you in the House," she informed him as she dressed.

"I have a penis to maintain!" he retorted, grabbing her by the waist and tossing her on the bed, his face hovering just barely over hers. "Please don't leave…yet. I want you."

"This is the best you can do?" she joked, and then continued, "I want *you* too, but I have to go, really. We're too old for a quickie. Save it for this Sunday."

"This Sunday?" he asked, bewildered, lifting his weight from her half-clothed form.

"Yes, this Sunday. Sunday is when I'll be returning to Austin."

"Where do we meet?"

"Here, of course. Besides we have a kitten to feed!"

"Oh, I forgot."

"Well I didn't. Something ate that chicken. And…when I was making the coffee I poked my head outside and saw it… it's a little black cat. He's so cute!"

"We should get some cat food."

"Yes!"

Rachael gathered her things. She kissed John David goodbye and was gone. Watching her car evaporate in the mist, he remembered that he had shut his phone off upon arrival the night before. There were several text messages and phone alerts. Tryphena had texted last night informing him that the speaker had cut them loose for Friday. Jessica had texted, as well as phoned. She was obviously back from "wherever," and checking up on her husband.

Entrusted to lock up, Dothan took his time. Pouring the last traces from the coffee pot into his cup, he set off into the dense, hilly wilderness. The scent of cedar pervaded the air. He noticed everything: the rocks, the stones, the pebbles; the scattered tufts of weeds and grasses; the sudden jutting live oaks and their recently molted, regenerated, light green leathery leaves. Then, from the far corner of his eye he caught it: a graceful yet fearful motion the color of pitch. Turning slowly, he met eyes with a very small, emaciated black cat. The yellow eye studied him distrustfully for an instant before vanishing into the fragments of the late morning's fog.

chapter sixteen

Dothan was not really interested in going back to district. Knowing that Jessica was around was the ultimate bummer. As usual, when she wanted something she would bombard him with messages. This was her pattern—had been for years—disappear for a month then show back up in a fury to communicate. He was so sick of it all. As he drove back to his apartment in Austin, he fanaticized about divorcing her. His fantasy was shattered when the realization that his livelihood would be severed as well. In Texas, State Reps. make $600 a month. One cannot make a living on that. While the system may have worked in the horse and buggy era, now, the structure of the State Legislature largely ensured that only the rich and connected could play. No, he would not ask Jessica for a divorce.

He tried to chill at his apartment and wait for the lunch hour rush to dwindle before getting back on the road. Out on the patio, he sat smoking, drinking and thinking. *What had just happened?*

This experience with Rachael had nudged awake a forgotten nook somewhere in the man. Dothan was an artist. His artistry had always expressed itself most definitively through words. Words were his canvas, his colors. This nook was so remote within the man that even when wandering into it, as he had this morning exploring the foggy hillside, he did not notice—although it was right before his eyes.

Dothan was certainly a Texan. It permeated from his presence. If one were to overhear him speaking in an airport anywhere in the world they would probably say to themselves, 'now there's a Texan.' He could be wearing Middle Eastern robes, it would not matter—he was a Texan. But Texas was far too young a place on the map to adequately bespeak his pagan soul. This experience with Rachael had nudged awake a forgotten nook in the man.

Traffic had, for now, absconded. Still, he did not wish to make the trip back home. He did not wish to return his wife's call. Instead, he called his Capitol office and got the response he wanted: the answering machine. *Had Tryphena not come in today? Who knows.* At this point in the session there was always so much to do. But the coast was clear. He would be alone…he hoped.

So to kill even more time, he went into work. The place was largely a ghost town. Once safely in his office, the desk looked like a disaster area. Newspapers and mail were everywhere. He sat at the computer and surfed different news sites. But he could not focus. As a digression, he brought up a site on Wordsworth, then Yeats. The origin of "The Rose of his Memory" was coming back into focus. *Had a fine beam found the concealed nook?* He wondered.

Still, he couldn't concentrate. He wanted to call Rachael. *But should I?* His restlessness was getting the best of him; his unease rooted in the pending communication with his wife.

Fed up with sitting on the fence, he decided to just show up at the house; making an excuse as to why his phone didn't work; that he had lost his charger or something. *Perhaps I'll catch her with her lover,* he mused. *Then all would be settled.* Once home, he knew he would need a distraction or, *be stuck listening to her nonsense.* He opened his briefcase and pushed in a pile of mail.

~

The house was barely lit, either on the outside or inside, when he arrived. The whole situation was awkward. Jessica was sitting on the back patio deck, drinking wine and talking on the phone. From the darkness below he heard the rumbling of waves. Dothan stood over her where she sat on a lounge chair. A mild gulf breeze was blowing in. The air smelled of stale salt.

"Well, speak of the devil Jeanie, it is JD!" Jessica spoke into the phone while looking up at her husband. "Jeanie says 'hi,'" she said, cupping the phone speaker.

"I don't know why he didn't call me back. I intend to find that out. OK, I'll call you tomorrow. See ya' girl."

"That was Jeanie, JD."

"I gathered that," he said, looking out into the invisible Gulf.

"Why didn't you call me back? I left several messages."

"I can't find my phone charger. My phone is dead."

"Damn, your ass looks good in those jeans. Have you been working out?"

"Maybe," he replied, turning around.

"Damn. I thought I was gonna be able to have a conversation with that butt. Your face spoiled it."

Dothan could not help but laugh. Then he stopped laughing. "So where were you this time?"

"Where was I? Like I told you, California, I was out there seeing my aunt. She just got remarried you know."

"No, I didn't know, because you never tell me shit. You just split."

Jessica, rose from her chair and approached JD in her customary 'let's fuck now' fashion.

Dothan was not interested.

"It's the black girl isn't it?"

"What the fuck are you talking about?"

"Try-Try-Try-…"

"Tryphena, Goddamnit! Her name is Tryphena!"

"Whoa! I hit a button, didn't I?"

"I'm not sleeping with Tryphena, if that's what you're talking about. My God, she's half my age, at least."

"Why can't we just have fun JD?" Why do you have to make everything so lame?"

"I'm not doing anything." Dothan could no longer take the mind games. "I'm going into the den where I'm going to try and find something decent to watch on satellite—which will most likely be difficult. If you would like to join me, you are welcome."

Regretting his invitation, the two struggled through a commercial-broken version of *Hi Fidelity.* What was strange to Dothan was the fact that earlier that day he was in Dripping Springs with

Rachael. *Where is she now?* He longed to call her. The idea of her with her husband, Donald, was suddenly inflicting pain. It was like a terrible memory, which having been blocked out, suddenly flashed before him as if for the first time.

Somehow, he escaped having to have sex with Jessica. *Perhaps she felt the same way?* he considered. But he didn't really care at this point. *Good actually*, he thought. At bed time the two went their separate ways as was customary.

~

Dothan awoke to the smell of breakfast wafting-in from down the hall, which was odd, as Jessica rarely prepared food of any kind anymore. His first thought was that perhaps she had hired a new maid, who actually cooked. However, as he emerged from the long cedar hallway, he discovered that the ravenous odor was, indeed, being orchestrated by his wife.

"What the hell is this?" Dothan asked, still half asleep.

"It's called breakfast. There's fresh coffee in the pot by the way."

Even odder, he thought. "What's the occasion?" he said, pouring a cup.

"What are you talking about JD?" Jessica asked, flipping the bacon.

"What am I talking about? Since when do we eat breakfast together – particularly with you cooking it?"

"I woke up hungry. What can I say? What makes you think I'm making enough for you, anyway?" She retorted with a sly smirk.

"Do I need to hit Whataburger again?"

"I'm just kidding, JD"

Dothan sat down at the table and began nursing his cup of coffee. "I found your charger, by the way."

"What?" he asked, confused, taken off guard.

"I found your charger. It was in your old briefcase. You really need to get a new one. I know it was your father's, but that thing is outdated."

"What were you doing going through my briefcase, Jessica?"

"There's a letter in there from Harry Spencer."

"What? You went through my Capitol mail?"

"Yes, I went through your Capitol mail. There's a letter from Harry Spencer in it."

"Ok, so what?"

"Aren't you interested in what he might be writing to you?"

"Not really, I think the guy's a sicko, frankly."

"I am JD; if it were me, I would be interested."

"Well, Jessica, you are not me."

Breakfast was served and the two sat down at the kitchen table as a family unit for the first time in…*how long?* he wondered.

"Daddy's not very happy with you by the way," Jessica commented out of nowhere.

"Let me guess…the Brazoria deal?" Dothan questioned, agitated, through a mouthful of eggs.

"So, as well as sleeping with a young black woman, you're a mind reader too—with bad manners."

"What? Would you quit fucking with me about that? I'm not sleeping with…," Dothan paused for an instant, then finishing his sentence, "with anyone."

"Had to think about that for a second, didn't we?"

"So your father is unhappy?" Dothan forced.

"Well, it's not so much that he is pissed, it's the officials in Brazoria that are miffed. And if they're not happy, then he's not happy. There's even talk about getting someone—a Brazoria Republican—to run against you. They are the largest county in your district, you know."

"I think I know my district. Fuck them."

"Will that be printed on the official mail out?"

"I explained the hold up to your dad. If he plays ball then the sooner we get what we want. If he resists, then he's fucked. It's that simple. I explained that to him."

"But you didn't explain that to the county, did you?"

"I guess I should make an appointment and go over there."

"Ya' think?"

"Don't worry your pretty little head? Your daddy won't see his 'investment' squandered."

"Do you really think it's pretty?"

"What?"

"I knew you were just being a sarcastic asshole, JD."

Dothan was at a loss for comment, at least not a positive one. Jessica might still be an attractive woman, but all her imperfections were exaggerated in the man's embittered eyes. What he saw now was only a jail keeper.

The two went into Houston; again, for the first time in a

long time. As they visited the Museum of Fine Arts, they nearly bonded while appreciating a Kandinsky collection on loan. Later, at the Rothko Chapel they held hands; the strange oil-black canvases meditating indifferently before them. For a brief time Dothan seemed happy. Perhaps remembering the days of his youth when women were many. For a brief time, Jessica had been one of those women. Then reality reminded him that she was now his wife.

The whole day was simply surreal. The man's mind was troubled, deeply troubled.

~

Later that night, back at the beach house, the tired representative retired to his study. As he emptied his briefcase of the Capitol mail, he happened upon the letter from Harry Spencer. He had forgotten about it. He sliced the envelope open with his ivory handled letter opener, a family heirloom, and removed the contents. Unfolding the parchment colored paper, it struck him as offensive that a man as disgraced as Harry would still find it appropriate to use official State letterhead. He was certain it was meant as a personal insult, and he took it as such. He moved the lamp closer and read the single page. Before he was half finished he found himself pitying the man who wrote the letter. When finished, he refolded the letter and slipped it carefully back in its envelope.

He checked his email and saw that Tryphena had forwarded a message from the Select Joint Committee on Immigration Reform, Committee Clerk. Apparently they were having a meeting this next week. The immigration bill was still stalled and something needed to be done. Dothan knew what that meant; he and Rachael would be back on the proverbial runway again. He did not mind this at all. Something in the correspondence, however, struck him as strange: they would be reviewing two new bills. *Two new bills?* The filing deadline had passed. *How is this possible? What is Reed up to?* Dothan's thoughts returned to the letter from Harry.

There can't be anything to it, could there? Of course not, Dothan concluded. Dothan suspected that Harry was not just a pedophile, but a paranoid schizophrenic as well. *Maybe Reed Jackson had undermined him, so what.* But the other material found therein was to his mind: *simply nuts.* He understood this was an obvious attempt to discredit the work they were doing in the Select Joint Committee.

Dothan found all of this bullshit boring. He allowed his mind to turn towards more pleasant things. He took a few puffs off a joint he had stashed in his desk and now wished to hear the voice of his 'Rose.' Although stoned, Dothan was not so much a fool as to dial her number; instead he texted her to determine her status.

Dothan: What's up? Can you talk?

He did not have to wait too long before he got a response.

Rachael: Not now. Eating with the family.

Dothan suddenly felt jealous, envious of her husband. His high was sinking lower.

Dothan: When? I really want to talk to you.

Rachael: Not now. Eating with family!

His depression was turning to anger.

Dothan: WHEN!

Rachael: Can't make tomorrow at the cabin.

Dothan: What! Call me – something!

He craved a cigarette and quietly slipped out onto the back patio balcony.

Jessica, complaining about her back, had gone to bed. He did not want to wake her. Smoking, he waited for a response from Rachael.

He waited.

He waited.

He had inhaled nearly half a pack and felt frustrated. He longed to talk to her, but knew that he needed to let it go—then—in a bizarre act of self-control, he hurled his phone into the Gulf of Mexico.

~

Sunday morning found him in remorse. He sauntered into the kitchen where the only smell that loitered was that of coffee; he languidly poured a cup as if it were a vocation he had long ago tired off.

"Good morning, JD," Jessica said from the den.

"Morning."

"What's wrong with you?"

"Nothing," he said. He entered the den and sat in his lazy boy.

"What time did you turn in last night?"

"I don't know. I went through my mail after you went to bed."

"Did you read Harry's letter?" she asked, perking up.

"Yeah, it was nothing. I actually feel sorry for that sad fuck."

chapter seventeen

Dothan sat disengaged while Chairman Reed Jackson went about the committee room, ranting about everything from the Federal Government to the Select Joint Committee's inability to get the only bill they had produced, thus far, out and onto the House and/or Senate floor for a vote. Although the immigration bill had finally been voted out of its respective House committee (it was basically dead in the Senate), it was now stalled on the House calendar. This meant the bill still would not get to the floor for a vote. For Dothan, this sounded like a morass of convoluted nonsense. *It's a good bill*, he reasoned, *so what's the problem?* Of course the fact that it had made it out as far as it had in the House could be largely credited to Ron Martinez and Dothan. The fact that it had essentially died in the Senate was both a reflection on the ineffectiveness of Rachael, as well as a repudiation of Reed.

Again, Rachael was absent. Her absence had become the norm, and this both angered and depressed Dothan. Today,

Reed had made his customary excuses on her behalf. Dothan couldn't help feeling, as the chairman battered the room, that a disproportionate degree of his swings were directed at him. But as usual, his thoughts were repeatedly on other things—his thoughts were on Rachael. *Where is she?* She still had not texted or called him since he had tossed his phone in the Gulf. He had purchased a new phone and texted, as well as called her with his new number. Dothan was beginning to suspect that the high of destroying phones had a disproportionately protracted low.

Reed bellowed for what seemed like forever, but in fact was only an hour. This was a side of Senator Jackson that Dothan had never seen. Yes, the chairman was definitely a bully; it was ingrained in his DNA, but his demeanor heretofore had always been as dispassionate as a surgeon's. Luckily, when finished discussing the immigration bill, his tone grew more subdued. He asked if anyone had any questions. No one did. It was time to move on.

"As you all know," Reed continued, "in the email we sent out, there are several new bill proposals that we need to address. This is a tactic I have used in the past and have found it most effective. If the House does not get our immigration bill out on the floor for a vote before the end of session, I will demand the governor call a Special Session in order to do so. Perhaps this will do the trick. I feel comfortable the bill will pass once out. If it does not pass, or they refuse to place it on the calendar at all, it will be a decision they will regret. For if we go to Special Session, what will be momentarily before you, the committee, will be on the Special Session agenda as well. The message:

'Do what we wish because we will get what we want either way. If you resist it will only make matters worse.'"

The committee clerk now began passing out packets to all the committee members.

"Are we sure the governor is on board?" a representative asked.

"The governor will do as I say," Reed insisted and the questioning member shrank in his chair. "I now ask you to open your packet and begin reviewing the materials therein."

Dothan did just that. What he found was quite strange. Within the packet there were two bill drafts: the first, relating to the coinage of an emergency currency; and the second, relating to an emergency voluntary division of the Texas Rangers.

What is this?

Chairman Jackson excused himself to answer a call. The committee members were left to their respective meditative states. Dothan was something of a speed-reader, and after blazing through the series of texts, he looked up questioningly at Ron. Ron looked nervous.

Reed reentered and signaled to Representative Martinez, who subsequently rose from his chair, excused himself and left the room.

This is becoming a habit, Dothan thought.

The chairman then adjourned the committee. "We will meet to discuss these two bills next Monday. I am relying on everyone's discretion. This information is confidential! Please inform your respective staffs of this, as well." The members vacated the meeting.

Striding the bustling hallway back to his office, Dothan discovered Rachael, an armful of files under her arm, hurrying towards him in the opposite direction.

"Oh my Lord, is it over?" she asked, panting; stopping him.

"Yeah, Chairman Creepy just let everybody go. Where the hell have you been?"

"Matthew has strep. I had to get him in to see the doctor. It's been a nightmare. The poor boy can hardly swallow. Donald is being such an asshole. I called Reed. Did he not tell ya'll?"

"He said you were detained on a family matter."

"What was the discussion about?"

"Well, he bitched at everyone about our ineffectiveness."

"Did he say anything about the Senate version of the bill?"

"Only that it was stalled."

"Shit, yes it is. I think some of those old bastard senators are just plain jealous. They'll pass it—it's just going to have to be the House version. You got it as far as calendar; congratulations."

"Well, now I have to schmooze them."

"You can do it, John David…you're a rockstar."

This flattered Dothan. His mind was suddenly racing between the past and present.

"I can't stop thinking of you," he said.

"I can't stop thinking of you," she concurred. "I'm so sorry about blowing you off last night. It's just…"

"I understand. Don't worry about it."

"But I have to go out to the cabin as soon as possible, I need to feed that kitten."

"I saw him!"

"What, you saw him?"

"Yes. After you left, I walked the brush around the house. I saw him, a black cat. It's very skinny."

"See, we have to go out there!"

"Can we go tonight?"

"Yes. It'll have to be later. I can't get away until sometime after ten."

The House bell could be heard ringing, calling Dothan to his duties. "I have to split! I'll see you tonight. You got my text with my new number didn't you?"

"Yes, what happened to your phone, John David?"

"I've got to go!" he shouted, turning his head over his shoulder, while pacing quickly away.

The House schedule was now in full crunch mode. Bills were stacking up wherever Dothan looked: on the floor, in committees. Lobbyists who were under the gun to justify their exorbitant salaries, accosted anyone who would listen. Over in the Senate, the workload was so immense that staff sometimes stayed until after midnight regardless of the floor schedule.

There was still two months to go until *Sine Die*.

Under these circumstances, the two promptly began a clandestine love affair. Just two weeks in and they were now largely commuting from the cabin.

~

With a solitary candle quivering on the dresser, Dothan lit a cigarette, and then, leaning over, lit Rachael's with his cigarette's cherry. The two had just caught their breath. They were enjoying the sex that only those freshly in-love enjoy; the kind of magical lovemaking that projects the illusion that life is a beautiful adventure; with no knowledge that the vessel that carries it on its way is almost surely to end up decimated on a cold and rocky shore. This is the folly of youth. But neither was young.

"I'm diggin' this cigarette," Dothan mumbled, exhaling a vortex of smoke.

"I can't believe I'm smoking. Look what you're doing to me, John David."

"Well, you do look silly trying to inhale."

"Shut up!" she retorted, in between coughs. Reaching for a glass of water that sat on the nightstand, she drained what was left, then deposited the half-smoked cigarette in it. "Chairman Creepy," she said out of the blue.

"What?"

"Chairman Creepy," she repeated, "that's funny."

"He is creepy. That dude's a freak, and a dick. How can you be friends with that guy?"

"We're not really friends, John David, we're associates. He's not all that bad."

"Compared to whom, General Pinochet?"

"That's ridiculous. Reed was my mentor. He took me in and showed me the ropes. I owe all I have in the Senate to him."

"He probably just thinks you're hot."

"That's insulting, by the way. Besides, not everyone is a sex addict like you."

"I'm not a sex addict. I only think about sex when I'm with you."

"You are so full of shit." Rachael laughed…then stopped, "If only he could see me now, how disappointed he would be."

"Why? Well…maybe you're right. But it's only because people like him never really loved anything in their miserable life."

"That's not true, John David. He loved his wife, I'm sure of that. He has always spoken so nicely of her. It wounded him profoundly when she passed away. He loves God. He loves this country as well. He's a decorated veteran."

"That doesn't mean anything. Just because you've served doesn't mean you are some selfless martyr."

"What have you ever done that's selfless?"

"I let you go…all those years ago. I knew it was the right thing at the time…however much I hated leaving…I let you go."

"Oh, my love, that's sweet. I'm sorry." Rachael sat up from her side of the queen-sized bed and gently placed herself in John David's arms.

"I don't know how you can be a Republican," he blurted.

"Oh, John David, please," she pleaded, softly.

"I'm serious; I'm not trying to be mean. It's just…those people…they're artless squares. It's awful."

"Well, I can't argue, a guy like you would never survive a Republican Primary."

"You mean an artist-type?"

"You're not a 'type', you are an artist. And no, an artist has no place in our party."

"What makes an artist any different than an engineer or a manufacturer or a tech-geek? I mean, what do these people create? They're against everything. One could say that the nature of conservatism is anti-innovative, because they're hostile to new ideas. Look at the big tech guys, they aren't Republicans. If it were up to guys like Reed Jackson they're wouldn't be anything…not the ceiling of the Sistine Chapel…nothing!"

Rachael sat up, covering her large, pink-beige nipples with the bed sheet. "You may have a point," she retorted, clearly irritated, "but 'people' like you would trade basic jobs and food for 'art.' If the world were run by the likes of you, we'd all starve! What would that do to the state of art? Kind of hard to create when you can't lift your brush!"

"Damn woman," John David declared. "You sure are sexy when you're mad."

"Shut up. I have one thing to ask: Texas or Detroit?"

"Texas or Detroit, what the fuck are you talking about?"

"Texas is prospering, hell it could be its own country. Texas is conservative principals at work. Detroit…poor Detroit…is liberal principals at…or can I use the word 'work'? It really doesn't apply," she added sarcastically.

Dothan grabbed Rachael by the ankles, and thrusting her towards him, her head collapsing back down upon her pillow, he mounted her.

"I'm going to manufacture another orgasm in your beautiful body!"

"Really?" she said indignantly, but without a hint of protest. Rachael didn't resist. It wasn't long before the rogue representative accomplished his stated goal. But he was unable to match it within himself. The two, falling apart, repeated a session of panting. Only this time Rachael lay satisfied; John David frustrated.

"That's my art form."

"What?" she asked, confused.

"That's my art form. Not that I'm any good at it, but I'd trade all the museums in the world for this. There is nothing more beautiful. I love making you cum. The look in your eyes… the movements of your face…the quivering of your body…I'd trade it all." With this conclusion he turned on his pillow and looked in her satisfied eyes. There was not a trace of detectable guilt behind them. The poet in him knew that this would not last. But the poet in him refused to accept this.

The two infidels fell asleep in each other's arms.

Rachael awoke sometime later to the imploring cry of a kitten. She had placed food out for the stray that evening upon arrival. She was worried that something else might have eaten the food. Gazing at the clock, she surmised it was nearing the time she must rise; and did so. She sat on the stone bench, which sat on the cusp of the surrounding brush, as the first splashes of day became visible. She drank her coffee and tried to coax the barely visible creature, just out of reach, that squatted both trusting and terrified.

The sun was well up before John David awoke. After grabbing a cup of coffee, he searched the cabin for Rachael. He saw her through the window, sitting on the edge of the yard.

Hearing the creak of the door, Rachael turned from where

she sat and shushed Dothan with her index finger. He immediately knew why. Softly he traveled the stones that lead in her direction. From behind a cactus, a small black head could be detected. As Dothan came closer, he could see it was ferociously lapping up a bowl of wet cat food.

"What do you think we should call him?" Rachael asked softly.

"Um…how about…Carson?" Dothan said, conscious of his volume.

"Carson, I like that. Carson the kitty. Carson it is. Carson, meet your new daddy."

Dothan stood, shivering in the morning coolness, wearing only his underwear and a t-shirt. As he watched Rachael look lovingly and longingly at the kitten as it licked its lips and whiskers, he could not control the tears that ran down his cheek. Ashamed, he turned back towards the cabin.

~

Several hours later, the two parted, both heading back to the Capitol. Dothan chugged down the highway listening to Foster and Lloyd's second album, *Faster and Louder*.

Rachael, racing in her convertible and listening to Austin radio, received tragic news about an estranged former colleague.

chapter Eighteen

I.

Dothan strolled into the Capitol in the best of moods. He was completely oblivious to the news that was snaking its way through the halls. With a song in his head and a step as light as a feather, he entered his office. Tryphena was kneeling at the filling cabinet as the door swung open.

"JD, have you heard?"

Dothan stood clueless.

"It doesn't look like you've heard," she said, excitedly, and stood up.

"I have no idea what on earth you are talking about. What is it that I was supposed to hear?" he asked. He rushed passed her and entered his office.

Tryphena followed him in. "Good, you're sitting."

"What the hell's going on around here?"

She closed the door behind her and took a seat in front of Dothan's desk. "Harry Spencer is dead."

"What?" Dothan asked, stunned.

"An apparent suicide."

"Jesus Christ, I knew that dude was fucked up. I guess it was all just too much for him."

"What was too much?"

"Life."

"Well, the way he died is pretty weird."

"How did he die?"

"Auto-erotic asphyxiation."

"You mean where you jerk off with a belt around your neck?"

"That's disgusting, JD. Yes…, I think it's something like that."

"Well maybe it was an accident."

"Apparently there was a note."

"Big surprise."

"What do you mean?"

"Ah…nothing. I'll tell you sometime. All I can say is that the late Harry Spencer was one sick, sad son-of-a-bitch."

"Yes, he was."

"So what's on the agenda for today?"

"Before we get started, have you realized that you haven't shaved? You're working some serious five o'clock shadow there, and it's not quite ten a.m."

Dothan ran his palm over the stubble on his face. "Shit! I guess I forgot!"

"That's a first. If nothing else, you're usually well groomed."

"Yeah…" Dothan felt vulnerable, sensing that Tryphena knew where he had been. "What do you think I should do? I have to be on the floor in a less than twenty minutes."

"Well, your hair is getting longer—are you planning on getting a haircut?"

"I don't know, I was thinking of growing it out a little."

"Just go with it, at least for today. You're a rebel, that's obvious. Besides, all that black hair goes great with those big circles under your eyes."

"Yeah, I didn't get much sleep last night. I was up reading bills."

At this moment Pam opened the door and entered his office. "Excuse me, sir."

"Yes Pam, what is it?" Dothan answered, irritated.

"Senator Jackson is here to see you."

"What?"

"Yes, sir."

"OK. Ask him to give me a moment."

Pam left the room with the door wide open. Dothan and Tryphena sat somewhat bewildered. "What do you think he wants?" Dothan whispered.

"We're about to find out."

"Tell him to come in."

Tryphena vacated the office, and after greeting Senator Jackson, sent him back to see Representative Dothan.

"Welcome, Senator Jackson. Please take a seat," Dothan said, rising from his chair.

"Oh, please Representative Dothan, it is not necessary to get up."

"What can I do for you, sir?"

"Well sir, actually there is something you can do for me," Reed said, taking a seat.

"OK. Name it."

"I'm sure you've heard, Harry Spencer was found dead this morning."

"Yes, that was brought to my attention—terrible, truly tragic. I know that the two of you were friends from way back."

"Yes, indeed," he replied, visibly upset. Reed continued, "No doubt the press will solicit a response from you. They are eternally in search of something nasty. I would appreciate it if you would handle it like a gentleman. His legacy is what I am concerned about."

"Legacy, sir?"

"Yes, legacy." Late Representative Spencer was a brilliant legislator and attorney. He authored some very good laws."

"Yes, sir," Dothan replied out of courtesy.

"All I ask is that, if you are approached by the media and they ask for a comment…"

"I will handle it like a gentleman, sir. I have no ax to grind with Harry. In fact, I can't help but feel pity for the man. I will say something honorable, I assure you."

"Thank you." The strained expression on Reed's face was that of one who needed to cry but was restraining it desperately. "Good day, Representative Dothan. And good job with the House version."

"Thank you," Dothan replied, somewhat amazed that Reed would lower himself down to the level of acknowledging him.

Reed Jackson rose to leave, but before he crossed the threshold of Dothan's door, he turned and commented, I believe you are in need of a shave, sir."

"I am aware of this."

"Well then, good day."

The House bell was again clanging, calling him to his duty. After Reed had left his office he regretted that he had not asked about the two other bills that the SJC members were given yesterday.

Tryphena entered as he pondered his regret. "So what was that all about? I tried to eavesdrop."

"Oh nothing, he's worried about Harry Spencer's 'legacy.'"

"What legacy—a legacy of perversion?"

"I don't know," Dothan answered, gathering his bill books. "So what's on the agenda today—anything I need to know?"

"I had Pam put all my notes in there. You are good to go."

"Rock-n-Roll."

II.

Back at the cabin the two infidels lay naked, once again. But as this was the weekend, and neither chamber was meeting, they had the convenience of slumbering into the morning. The couple would lie naked for hours after lovemaking, just talking and talking. This pillow talk was the pattern.

"I feel like I'm from Mars," Dothan stated, inhaling his cigarette at an accelerated rate.

"I have no idea what you could possibly be referring to," Rachael replied as she sat on the edge of the bed and cleaned herself with a damp cloth.

"Ray Bradbury."

"What about Ray Bradbury?"

"*The Martian Chronicles*, did you ever read that book?"

"I can't remember," she responded, placing her head on his naked chest."

"I love the smell of your hair. It's like wood smoke and chocolate."

"What? You are really confusing me, John David."

"Your hair, that's what it smells like to me."

"Only you would come up with that." She fidgeted a little until she was comfortable, then asked, "Now, what about the *Martian Chronicles*?"

"Ah yes, the *Martian Chronicles*: The civilization that the earthlings find when they land on Mars, it's the perfect balance between art and functionality—like Yeats' Byzantium, but even more beautiful: Glass houses that rise in perfection, and books where the pages are like slivers of silver."

"Sounds nice."

"That's what I mean: Sometimes I feel like I'm from Mars, like I have nothing in common with the human race. In the book, the humans take pleasure in destroying their works."

"Of course," Rachael concluded, lifting her bare form off John David and then excusing herself to the bathroom.

Shortly afterward, the two resumed this ritual.

"Speaking of works, I was listening to some of those old tapes of yours. I was really struck by the song, "Centuries." It's such a great song, and being about vampires, I can't believe it wasn't a hit."

"It was in the middle of the Grunge era and I could sing, really sing— not that some of those early Seattle bands weren't bad ass— but I could really sing. This was the problem."

"I suppose you're right; you would know better than I. But it's the lyrics, too,…they are so…insightful. You really paint a believable character. How does it go?"

"I don't know; you tell me," Dothan answered, slyly, enjoying the flattery.

"OK, hang on…" Rachael had to conjure the tune in her head, which took a moment, "*Dusty Latin books and clergy crooks, have condemned me through the ages. Slaves from ebony sages, to Red wages…all I have seen, in their presence I have been. Consumed with sin, but what is that today? I've witnessed the West spread then fray. Shake spirit for clay, an aloof bystander…to their philandering, their petty scandalling's –oh oh. The fools, the criminals I've seen dignified.*'"

"Bravo." Dothan clapped while holding his lighter, a smoke hanging from his mouth.

"Wait, I haven't yielded the floor."

"Excuse me, Madame Senator."

"Let me recite the chorus: '*A villain in the past, a stranger to today. My mouth it plays a pretender song with the wine I sip from your navel. What I'd give, what I'd give…for a taste of running you, before the morning…dew.*'"

"Damn, I don't think I even remember all of that and I wrote the thing."

"Those are great lyrics! And the talking part?"

"You mean the bridge?"

"Yes the bridge. '*All has failed, and all will fail. Can I sip from your sleek grail, poised so frail in its waiting? And on your blood like balm, baby we'll sail, through my hopeless world without walls.*' Then to end with that line, what is it?"

"Do you mean, '*two roses upon your throat*'?"

"Yes! That is an awesome line."

"Thank you. If you represented the record buying public in 1995, my life would've taken a considerably different course."

"Yeah, I'm sorry John David," Rachael lamented, resuming her place on his chest and caressing the hairs girding his nipple with her fingers.

"It's cool; it's all meaningless in the end."

"I don't see how you can live believing that."

"I'm surprised you like 'Centuries.' I bet Reed Jackson would condemn you."

"You're probably right, but I wouldn't care what he thought." Rachael wanted to change the subject, so she drifted back to what they had only briefly touched on earlier, after a few dramatic cursory comments, "It's a shame about Harry."

"Yes it is." Just then Dothan remembered the letter Harry had sent, "Oh my God!"

"What is it?" she asked alarmed.

"Remember I told you earlier that Harry had sent me a letter on State letterhead?"

"Yes, I also remember you didn't want to talk about it."

"Can you forgive me for wanting to hold your beautiful naked body over discussing a letter from Harry Spencer?"

"You are forgiven."

"Like I told you, Harry credited Reed for hiring Warren Jenkins."

"Right; it is a bit peculiar that Reed had him on the payroll simultaneously with you and Harry's race—if that claim is even accurate. Have you tried getting in touch with Warren Jenkins?"

"I have Tryphena looking into both the Campaign Finance Reports as well as getting in touch with Warren. He's kind of disappeared. He won't answer our phone calls."

"That's odd, you were his client. You paid him didn't you?" she asked, rhetorically.

"Yes, of course I paid the expensive bastard, but that's not all that the letter said."

After revealing the extent of Harry Spencer's final, official, known correspondence, Rachael agreed with John David that the man was disturbed, even perhaps a little jealous.

"Well, may God have mercy on his soul," Rachael added, forlornly.

"He killed himself; doesn't that mean he burns in hell for eternity?"

"Perhaps."

"What a fucked up religion. I don't know how you believe in something like that."

"Christ is the only redemption. Man will always fail, like your song states. I couldn't live in this horrible world if I didn't believe. You are such a nihilist—it is a product of your vanity. I wish you believed."

"Why, so I could feel guilty about sleeping with you like you do with me?"

This callous comment hurt Rachael deeply, and a tiny space in her heart that she had reserved exclusively for John David, died from his speaking it.

~

Rachael, as was her habit regardless of where she found her bed, awoke at dawn. As customary, John David slept into the morning hours. The infidels had planned on spending Sunday together, but as Rachael sat watching the fattening Carson lap his food in the awakening spring morning, she could not refrain from feeling anger towards her lover.

Because she felt the need to check her cell phone, she had brought her purse outside with her. Fortunately, nothing of an urgent nature was to be found. As she dug through her Coach handbag, she found her photo album. *It's funny*, she thought, as she began flipping through the pictures, funny that something as simple as a tangible photo album was now something of an anachronism.

Although she wished she were younger, she could not help but feel pity at the irony of the Millennial Generation, for they would be left with very little records of themselves. Their entire lives, recorded to the point of absurdity, existed in an eternally changing cloud; they had nothing concrete. Technology would change and the majority of these records would vanish like the music on an 8-Track cassette.

She paused at the pocket-sized portraits of her two children and felt an odd sense of joy tinged with pain. They were hers, but were not hers. Her husband, Donald, was detached; *would that be the case if they were his own flesh and blood?* she wondered. Long ago, she had wished to share that experience with John David. But he was not interested. She did not take it personally really, as he had never had any children of his own. Still, the anger she felt was growing. She quietly gathered her things and secretly left.

~

When John David finally rose, he found only a lukewarm pot of coffee. Rachael was absent. He called her repeatedly on her cell.

Repeatedly he got only her voicemail.

chapter Nineteen

Dothan was down in the dumps. Something was obviously wrong with Rachael. *But what could it be?* he wondered.

As Monday rolled around, he found himself committed to attend the Select Joint Committee meeting, but he could not commit to it. The more intensely he longed for Rachael, the less obligated he felt to everything else, particularly his present responsibilities. His extant quest was now Rachael. He had felt the gnawing sting of a broken heart before; Rachael being his first. Instinct and experience told the man that perhaps he was on the brink of one again. Something he had sworn to himself, years ago, would never happen again.

A thin vein of hope that she might be at the meeting was the only impetus Dothan had for going, himself. He quickly discovered that she was absent. The chairman made no excuses on her behalf this time. It was more of the familiar ranting on Reed Jackson's part, more of fear and trembling on the committee's part.

Dothan just sat there, dejected and listened.

"To answer your question," Reed said, addressing an inquisitive member of the committee, "a bill is eligible for consideration even if it is filed beyond the deadline, *if* the governor deems it of an urgent nature. I've no doubt that our executive will agree with me that, given the continued forced devaluation of our dollar, an emergency coinage bill is of an urgent nature. I've no doubt that our executive will agree, given the continued threats of terrorism by the Mexican cartels, coupled with the continued ineptitude of the Feds, that an expansion of the Texas Rangers is of an urgent nature."

The minute the committee adjourned, Dothan vanished. The day's floor schedule was insane and he needed to try and get his act together. He needed to consult with Tryphena. But the immediate need to see Rachael was starting to eat him alive.

Instead of taking the short hallway that lead to his office, he took the long hallway that lead to the Capitol proper. Once out of the crowded elevator, he paced his way through a throng of bodies, into Rachael's office.

"Is the senator available?" he asked the intern at the desk; his tone carried an air of impatience.

"No sir, she is not. Can I tell her that you came by?"

Dothan furiously studied the posh, Victorian, wood-ornamented office. He saw that Rachael's door was shut and hurriedly made his way towards it. The staff of Senator Logan gazed on in offended wonder as he jostled the locked door. This wonder was compounded by his pounding and pleading, "Are you in there? Damn it, are you in there!"

"Representative Dothan! She is not in there! Please, sir!" Logan's Chief of Staff implored.

"Open it."

"What?" the woman asked, her tone laced with pity.

"Open it! I want to see."

"Sir?"

"Open it, please," he calmly commanded.

"Get me the keys," the chief instructed her staff. She unlocked the door and stepped aside. A dark empty room with a neat vacant desk greeted Dothan.

"You see, sir…there is no one here."

"Where is she?" Dothan quizzed, his bloodshot eyes tinged with insanity.

"She's away on business and won't return for a day or so."

The wounded representative left Senator Logan's office, humiliated. During the entire trek back to the Capital Extension, he was wrought with a deep nausea, ignorant of the passersby acknowledging him. The route to his office seemingly took days not minutes. When he finally returned, it was obvious to everyone that something was not right.

Tryphena, in particular, was concerned. He sauntered past her with little more than a nod and retired to his private office, closing the door behind him. He collapsed into his chair and plunged his face into his hands; he thought of Robinson Jeffers: *'The wild God of the world is sometimes merciful to those that ask mercy, not often to the arrogant.'*

Dothan knew that he had lived a lifetime of arrogance. There is a part of nearly everyone, believer and atheist alike, who arrives at moral outrage towards something in this ugly world. He was conscious of his unworthiness. For only the second time in his life, he asked forgiveness from whatever invisible force governed this universe, be it God or chance. Still, his implacable vanity would not accept absolution. Only one force in the cosmos had that authority.

Dothan was shaken from this self-absorption by a knock at his door. After acknowledging it, Tryphena entered. "JD, you've got a full plate today. There are a few things we really should go over."

"OK," he responded with an air of surrender.

"What's wrong?" she asked hesitantly, placing the stack of bill books before him.

"Nothing!" he shouted, rising from his chair, "These can fucking wait!" With this brash edict he thrust the stack of bill books from his desk. Pages and binding went flying, fluttering to the floor in confusion.

"JD, please!" Tryphena matched, both angry and concerned. "What is it? Is it that woman…that Senator…Rachael Logan?"

The defeated man fell back on his throne of defeat and from between the fingers that caged his ridiculous face, asked, "How did you know?"

"You really have your head up your ass, don't you?"

"What?" he questioned as if a bucket of cold water had been thrown over him.

"It's become obvious—at least to me. I just hope no one else sees it."

"I'm such a fool. Look at me! What a lack of dignity. You must think so little of me."

It was apparent that Dothan was in considerable pain, that both his heart and his ego were injured. She walked around his desk and stood over him like an adult consoling a child. She comfortingly, but cautiously, placed her hand on the base of his neck. He did not move from where he sat, his face still buried in his hands. A strange feeling came over Tryphena. It was that of flattery and disgust. Flattery: because he was exposing his nature to her in such a way. Disgust: because he was exposing his nature to her in such a way. A third emotion intervened within her on his behalf, that of compassion: The boy in the man…the man in the boy. It was this quality that had drawn women to him all his life. Tryphena was not immune.

With Dothan gradually rising from the ashes of his humiliation, the two sat and talked. Their discussion was removed from the legislation that scattered the floor. The talk was of Rachael Logan. Tryphena was half-jealous as Dothan spoke of his love for the lady senator. She had never known a man who could speak about such things, particularly as eloquently as he presently was. The tale of their relationship from long ago was unraveled in words so precisely placed that, for Tryphena, it was as if she were reading a novel. But it was the end that grabbed her profoundly.

"My God JD, you got her pregnant?" she asked bewildered. *So rich white people have to worry about things like this too?* she thought before cross-examining. "So what did ya'll do?"

"What could we do? There was no way she could have had the baby. We were eighteen. She was about to be a college girl, pledging a sorority. I was about to be a college boy. I had no money. We decided to have an abortion."

"She went for that? Isn't she hardcore Pro-life?"

"We'll no, she wasn't for it. In fact she begged me to consider the possibility of us having a baby together."

"How did you talk her into terminating the pregnancy?"

"I just asked her how her parents would take something like her being a teen mother—that I didn't really think that a baby right now was in their plans for her. That it didn't exactly work with the whole law school thing—especially with a rock-n-roller like me."

"So she went for it?"

"Yeah…she went for it." Dothan paused, and the look that draped over his face struck Tryphena to the bone. He continued, "I have made a lot of mistakes in my life. None so grave as that one."

"What do you mean? What happened?"

"The abortion got fucked up."

"What do you mean, 'fucked up?'"

"I mean it was a disaster. After it was done, she was infertile."

"What? How? How is that possible?"

"I'm not sure how. Apparently the instrument used to suck the baby out damaged her uterus. I'm not really sure to tell you the truth. She bled for several days. I'm such a piece of shit that I was more concerned with her parents finding out than anything else. I deserve all the suffering I have had to endure."

"You were only eighteen; you were young and foolish."

"I was a bad person. I *am* a bad person, Tryphena."

"You may be vain, but you are not a bad person, JD." Tryphena and Dothan looked at one another in the way that only true confidants are capable. She continued her questions, "So what happened after this?"

"We split up. All she left me with was a photo signed with a name I had begun to call her."

"Oh my God, that picture! *'The Rose of your Memory*!'"

"How did you know about that?"

"I found the photo in your volume of Shelley."

"Yes, my volume of Shelley; a favorite poet of ours."

"I'm sorry; it really was an accident, JD."

"Never mind, it's quite alright Tryphena," he said despondently. He continued his narrative, "She entered school here in Austin and I left for school down in San Marcos. She wanted nothing to do with me, really. She moved on. And I…I've never stopped loving her."

~

Regarding Rachael, silence begat silence. In his ailing guts, Dothan knew that she was gone. His misery was so absolute that he continued on with his obligations to the House in a sedentary fashion. But this stasis would be broken.

II.

"Ma' am?" Pam asked Tryphena as she sat at her desk, typing a press release for the local papers back in district.

"Yes Pam, what is it?" Tryphena asked without breaking her stare from the monitor.

"That man, Warren Jenkins, which you and Representative Dothan have discussed from time to time…"

"Yes?" Tryphena asked, impatiently.

"He called while you were at the Capital Grill."

"Really?" This piece of news peaked Tryphena's interest.

"Yes ma'am, he asked for Representative Dothan. He refused to leave a call back number."

"What did he want?"

"I don't know. He sounded strange, like he was stressed out about something."

"If he calls again, I don't care where I'm at—put him on hold—forever if you have to, but find me. I want to talk to him!"

"Yes, ma'am."

Warren Jenkins indeed called back. It was later that afternoon. Pam informed him that the representative was on the floor and would be for some hours; asking if he would mind if the Chief of Staff took the call. He agreed.

"Warren, how are you?" Tryphena asked, trying to control her excitement.

"I'm fine, I suppose. How are you doing Tryphena? Is the job I placed you in serving you well?"

Warren sounded stressed to Tryphena. "Things are great. I'm enjoying my first tour. I never got a chance to thank you."

"No need, dear. Listen, I haven't long to talk…"

"Where are you calling from, by the way?"

"From a pay phone."

"A pay phone? Where did you find one of those?"

"Believe me, it wasn't easy. But anyhow, I need to meet your boss. It's urgent. You are welcome to come as well…but I must warn you…the nature of this meeting is…is…is…," Warren's voice began to crack and shake.

"What's going on Warren?"

"When and where can we meet?"

"Anytime in Austin; you name it."

"Not Austin, it has to be remote. Somewhere out of the way."

"Why?"

"Where?" Warren softly demanded.

"I don't know…" Just then Tryphena thought of Dothan's District office near the beach in Matagorda. "How about our District Office?"

"In Matagorda?"

"Yes, you've been there, haven't you?"

"Sounds good. How about this Friday, say 10:00 p.m.?"

"I'll have to check with JD on that before we commit."

"Damn it Tryphena, I need a commitment now!" Warren pleaded.

Sensing the odd desperation in Warren's voice, Tryphena committed.

≈

Tryphena was worried about her boss. He was rapidly losing weight. He was showing up in the morning with a beer, and not one poured into a cup, but a beer in a longneck bottle. The office refrigerator was stocked to capacity…with beer. Dothan would leave the House floor and go to his office to kill a few, and then, return to the floor. He was doing very little to conceal it from staff.

Tryphena was both furious and sympathetic. *I wish I could comfort him. I wish that bitch would at least make contact. How weak, to disappear like she does. She's more worthless than some of the boyfriends I've had. They had the excuse of being poor. She's never suffered a day in her entitled life. If I wouldn't be removed from the Capitol by a legion of State Troopers, I would walk right into the Senate Chamber and knock the shit out of her.*

≈

Friday night rolled around and it was now time to depart for district. Tryphena insisted that she not only go, but that she drive as well. The lingering Hill Country cool was gradually enveloped by a heavy humidity the closer the two travelers came to their destination. Very little was discussed as the Mustang raced towards the Gulf. But what was discussed was the letter from Harry Spencer. Tryphena was shocked and offended, agreeing with JD that he was not only sick, but insane.

Dothan had brought along a Jim Croce CD, which he slipped into the slot; it played "Photographs and Memories" repeatedly.

Tryphena had to make numerous pit stops so JD could piss.

The small shopping center that housed the District Office was dark and vacant. A solitary street lamp set in the middle of the parking lot struggled to break the darkness. Not far removed from its feeble jurisdiction, a Jeep Cherokee idled in the shadows. Tryphena pulled up beside it and recognized Warren. She rolled down her window and greeted him, cautiously.

Dothan sat beside her half-drunk and fully detached.

"Hello Warren." Tryphena spoke, poking her head out the Mustang's window.

"Hello Tryphena, it's great to see you again. Hey JD!" he shouted at the silhouetted figure in the passenger seat.

"What do you say we take this meeting into the District Office?"

"Sure."

Upon exiting his Jeep, Tryphena observed that the political consultant cased out his surroundings with a degree of anxiety that was foreign to his character. Once inside, he requested the blinds be drawn. The three were sitting around a desk in the foyer.

"Jesus JD, you look like shit," Warren commented.

"You're still as chubby as ever," he retorted.

"JD," Tryphena scolded him.

"Oh, never mind Tryphena, I asked for it." Warren's smile was as phony as a modern pop singer's passion; his fidgeting belied the plasticity of his tone.

"What's wrong Warren? What's going on? Something isn't right."

"You can say that again."

"You want a beer?" Dothan asked him, pulling a cold one from a freshly purchased pack.

"No thanks, I've got to keep my senses about me."

"Why?" Dothan asked, still drunk and detached.

Sensing that Warren was uncomfortable with the situation, particularly Dothan's air, Tryphena took control of the conversation. "So Warren, recently I was going through campaign finance reports and discovered that you had ties to Reed Jackson. And, on the way down here, JD told me about this letter he received from Harry Spencer—a really fucked up letter. It gets a little out there, and quite unbelievable in places, but he accuses Senator Jackson of hiring you on behalf of JD. Is that bullshit as well?"

"Oh it's believable alright—all of it…every single unholy word." With this bombastic statement and his hands visibly trembling, Warren removed a parchment colored piece of folded paper from his back pocket. "Is this what you are referring to?" he asked Tryphena as he carefully unfolded it, placing it on the table before them.

"Oh my God! You got a letter too? JD, did you know about this?"

"What? Dothan questioned, taken off guard. He was now shaken from his lethargy. "Is that from Harry?" he asked, reaching for it. The letter was exactly the same as the one he had received. "What is this?"

"This is Harry's swan song, JD. You know what that is don't you?"

"Of course, but what of it? It's bullshit for the most part, right? The rantings of a lunatic pedophile?"

"I thought that myself, until Harry died.

"He committed suicide. He was going to be indicted," Tryphena stated, firmly.

"He wanted to die having an orgasm," Dothan interjected.

"JD, please!" Tryphena protested.

"The suicide note was planted. Harry was murdered."

"How do you know this, Warren?" Tryphena asked.

"The suicide letter was typed and signed with a signature stamp," Warren divulged.

"How do you know this?" Dothan inquired.

"The death occurred in Harris County. There is scarcely an elected official in Houston that I didn't have a hand in getting elected. All I had to do was put in a few phone calls."

"Is there any kind of investigation?" Tryphena asked.

"Not really. I think they just want it to go away."

"But why would anyone want to kill Harry Spencer?"

"You're looking at it Tryphena."

"You mean…the letter?"

"The two of you should be careful who you talk to. Don't mention this to anyone."

"I haven't. But if you got a letter, and I got one…who else did?"

"That's impossible to know, JD."

"So why are you telling us this if you don't want anyone to know?"

"You want to know Tryphena, I'll tell you why, because JD is part of the subject matter, and…I'm being followed."

"What?"

"That's right. And no JD, I haven't cracked up, so wipe that look off of your smug face." Warren remarked, causing Dothan to sit stiffly up in his chair. "I've been followed before, by sheriff's deputies and the like during heated campaigns…but this is different."

"How so?" Tryphena asked.

"Before, it was always just to intimidate. Whoever is following me is now looking for the right moment."

"The right moment for what?"

"I hesitate to say."

"Look!" Dothan interrupted, "What you've said is tripped out, but I don't buy it. Not the conspiracy bullshit. OK, so Reed figured out that his old army buddy was a perv, so he hired you to get someone to 86 him. That makes sense in the light of what's happened since summer."

"Since summer? But we first made contact at the beginning of last year—in January. You had just filed to run as a Democrat for this state rep seat that past December. By the way, no one thought you had a snowball's chance in hell to win."

This last comment chipped at Dothan's already wounded pride. "Well I did win, so fuck you."

"JD," Tryphena reacted, "all Warren's saying is it was *his* hit pieces on Harry that put you in the driver's seat."

"That's right Tryphena, hit pieces instigated by Reed Jackson. It's like all that's happened since then was in the pipeline beforehand. Reed knew Harry would be a liability if he were to win and then serve on the Select Joint Committee. So Reed, how did you put it JD…86'ed him?"

"Right."

"Reed knew that his plan would not work with a weak link. What Reed needed was an inexperienced puppet, with an inexperienced staff."

"That was me," Tryphena stated plainly.

"That was you, Tryphena."

"OK, so what's this…'plan?'" Dothan asked skeptically.

"What do you think is going on here with regards to the Select Joint Committee?"

"We're trying to regulate the anarchy from Washington," JD answered.

"To a degree, but not really. Think about it: an immigration bill that establishes agreements with states from another country; a coinage bill, meaning a currency; and lastly, an expansion of the Texas Rangers: a military. Then, if you look at the appropriation's bill that you voted for back in February, it allocated some eighty-five million for 'security purposes—' a border fence! What the hell do you think is being put into place here, JD?"

"They want to secede," Tryphena answered in lieu of Dothan's confusion.

"Bingo, they want to secede!"

"It's 1861 all over again! The South shall rise again!" Dothan declared, slamming his empty beer bottle on the table.

"Not quite, JD. This is not some racist nationalist movement of wackos; it's a calculated move. What instigated the Select Joint

Committee? The attack on the school bus! Yes, even a lazy, unin-formed population draws the line at charred little children."

"How did you know about the other two bills?" Dothan asked.

"I know everybody JD."

"OK, all this sounds very convincing, but that still doesn't prove what Harry states in his letter."

"No, it doesn't. But it sure points in that direction. I thought it bullshit too, until Harry died and I started being followed."

"Back to that," Tryphena jumped in, "what makes you think that you're being followed?"

"Well for one, I found a GPS tracker on my car. Then, my of-fice was broken into but nothing, and I mean nothing, was stolen. And at my home, which I haven't been back to since…" Warren became visibly upset.

"Since what?" Tryphena asked touched by this sudden display of emotion.

"My dog was killed."

"What? How?"

"According to the vet, he was poisoned."

"What, did the police say about all this?"

"The cops are worthless Tryphena, you should know that. They can't help with anything."

"So where are you staying Warren?" she asked.

"I float around motels. My ex-wife is up in Canada with my daughter. I sure as hell don't want to involve them. I just hope they're safe. I was calling all the time. My ex-wife was getting ir-ritated. I wouldn't tell her why I was calling. She would think me crazy. I ditched my cell and stopped calling her and nearly everyone else."

"What about Clark?" Dothan asked.

"Jack went to the UK a few months ago. He's working on some parliamentary campaign in England."

"England?" Dothan asked skeptically.

"Yes, England, JD; he worked in Mexico just out of school. Jack always had delusions of grandeur. He knows nothing. I want to keep it that way."

~

It was after midnight when the meeting broke up. Watching the red taillights of Warren's Cherokee trail out of the dark parking lot, Tryphena and Dothan sat discussing the evening with one another inside the crumbling Mustang.

"Well, I just don't buy it," Dothan concluded.

"I don't know either. Where to now, JD…it's late."

"Jessica is out of town. We can stay at my house."

chapter Twenty

The crack in the representative's skull was as wide as Palo Duro Canyon. In contrast, behind the eyes, a pressure was felt. While masturbating first thing this morning, upon climax, he was struck with a dizzy feeling that nearly knocked the man out. Now, Dothan's headache was so bad that he was having trouble dressing. This was more than a hangover.

The day before him stretched on in perpetuity. Not only did he have a full day on the floor, tonight there was a media event hosted by the *Texas Tribune*. While the dinner was being thrown in honor of the entire legislature, the *Tribune* had covered the Logan-Dothan Bill with enthusiasm. Rachael would be present. This filled him with both anticipation and dread. He felt like a man dying of starvation, being lead to the guillotine. He reached into his medicine cabinet and grabbed a bottle of Advil. He swallowed some dozen tablets and headed up South Congress towards the Capitol and into work. He had not eaten anything.

The day was dreadful, at least in his mind. Personal lives were altered for the good or for worse on the Texas House floor today, but Dothan paid little notice beyond his pressing a button signifying 'yes' or 'no.' The sawing teeth of unrequited love, or whatever it was, dug into his brain like maggots into a pine box. The world to him now smelled of rotting meat.

Down in his office, Dothan repeatedly filled his whiskey glass with cognac while changing into his tuxedo. Tonight's event started at seven and was within walking distance. Although it was now the month of May, surprisingly the weather was not yet unbearable. He strolled up Guadalupe, making his way towards the University of Texas campus. The smells of spring perfumed the early evening air. For a moment they disguised his disgust.

The AT&T Center was his destination, a brief trek that barely consumed two cigarettes. He claimed his name badge at the entryway table and headed straight for the bar. Remarkably, his journey was unimpeded by admirers, but he knew this wouldn't last.

With a whiskey in hand, he surveyed the large banquet room. His study for Rachael was broken every few minutes by partygoers seeking conversation. A master communicator, Dothan extricated himself with relative ease again and again. Reed Jackson and Ron Martinez were spotted first. Not too shortly there afterward, to Dothan's dismay, Donald Logan was seen. He killed his whiskey and needed another.

He watched the room from his place in line at the bar, through a buzz of bodies a red dress caught his eye. Although her back was to him, and she was on the other side of the great room, he had no doubt it was the Rose of his Memory. *'I'm left with a mind like a fuzzy hammer'* ricocheted around his doctored skull. Remembering the line from Jim Morrison, the poet not the rock star, Dothan could not help but chuckle. He was simply exhausted at this point. The floor had claimed his mind and Rachael his emotions. He was not yet drunk enough to confront her.

The seating arrangement concerned him. Dothan had not purchased a table, but he assumed Chairman Reed Jackson had. It was also assumed that he would sit with the Select Joint Committee on Immigration Reform. Standing in the bar line, yet again, he ran into Ron.

"Looking sharp JD, looking sharp—growing the hair out are we? I hear our bill will be on the floor next week. You are a professional ass kisser, my friend. I can't tell you how grateful I am that you are involved in this."

"I didn't buy a table, Ron, I only have an individual ticket which means I sit in open seating," Dothan interrupted, not interested in policy talk, "where are you sitting?"

"You're sitting with us, my friend. Reed has a table for our committee. I insist."

"Will there be enough room?" he asked, half longing to be seated near Rachael and half dreading it.

"Always room for you JD—beside, Senator Logan and her husband are sitting at the Right To Life table. There's extra room."

"Oh…really?" he questioned, rhetorically; his longing apparently greater than his dread.

❧

Dothan continued to drink through the night. He refrained from seeking out Rachael and she reciprocated, thus far. When the MC recognized elected officials, which took considerable time as there were so many present, Dothan did not stand when his name was announced. Instead, he sat staring into space, wondering how he would find a way to talk to her. He had to talk to her.

In the midst of conversation, from the corner of his blood-shot eye, he cased-out Rachael and her husband and waited for her to be alone. Then, Donald rose from his chair and headed toward the exit, his cell phone to his ear. Rachael got up as well, heading towards the bar. This was his chance!

Approaching her from behind, he tapped her naked shoulder. "Can I speak with you for a moment?" he asked, as she turned around, unsurprised.

"Of course, John David," she answered with a tone of formality as if they were on camera.

"Where's Donald?" he asked strategically.

"Oh, he had a business call. He might be gone all night," Rachael joked, without thinking.

"Let's get our drinks, shall we?"

Once the two had their adult beverages in hand, Dothan led Rachael away from the human thicket. Several times along the way the two were stopped and their photo was taken. The contrast could not have been more dramatic: Rachael with her kind, eloquent smile; Dothan with his somber mirror face like the cover of the *Best of the Doors*.

"So what would you like to talk about?" Rachael inquired, phonily.

"What?" he asked sickened by her plasticity. "What would I like to talk about...? What are you doing? Why are you doing it? Why won't you call me? What is going on?"

"Please John David, keep your voice down," Rachael begged through a smile. As she looked around the room, her breathing grew heavy. "John David, I'm sorry I haven't contacted you. I haven't known what to do. This has been eating at me every minute of every day. I'm sorry if I've hurt you, I just need some time to figure things out."

"Figure what out?"

"Us, the situation, what do you think?"

"What's there to figure out? I love you. You love me. What else is there? We were born to love one another."

"Please don't say things like that."

"Why, if it's the truth?"

"Because it complicates things even more."

"It doesn't complicate things at all, it simplifies them."

"You're not selling a bill John David...this is life. It affects others...other than just you."

"Don't fucking patronize me!" Dothan flared up.

"John David..."

"Quit calling me John David!" Dothan yelled. "My name is JD!"

"Please keep your voice down. People are looking. Can't we talk about this tomorrow? I'll call you. I promise."

"How about the cabin? I have so many things I want to tell you. You are the only one I can tell my soul to."

"Is our lovemaking a confessional?" Rachael snapped;

then realizing her transgression, changed her tone, "There's too much going on right now for that. Soon, I promise. We can talk tomorrow."

"I don't want to wait 'til tomorrow, I want to talk now. I want to have children with you."

"What, what on earth are you talking about?"

"We can adopt! I've always wanted a little girl! Let's adopt a little girl together! What about our little kitty, Carson, can't we adopt him?"

Rachael was on the verge of panic. This intimate discussion was ceasing to be intimate as those around the room started staring.

"You've had too much to drink John David. We can talk about these things tomorrow, please."

"JD Goddamnit, JD! It's two letters—TWO!" Dothan screamed, throwing his arms wide open to accentuate this point; the left hand hitting an hors d'oeuvre tray held by the waiter behind him. Bruschetta went flying, the waiter hit the floor. Losing his balance in the melee he had just instigated, Dothan tripped over the server and crashed into a Silent Auction display table.

Rachael stood aghast, her cover broken.

JD spent the rest of the night vomiting at his apartment; having left shortly after his accident. This 'accident' was witnessed by nearly everyone at the event; a certain lady senator's body language giving away their secret.

~

When Pam opened the office that next morning, Ron Martinez was waiting for her. Ron had pegged her as an outsider right away. If there was information to be had, she was the source. Inviting her to breakfast, the awkward Pam was so awestruck that she accepted with enthusiasm. As they sat in the Capitol Grill, Ron the attorney carefully cross-examined Pam the admin, flattering her at every turn. With what she divulged he was able to fill in the blanks.

Tryphena arrived shortly after the two had left for the grill. It seemed odd to her that Pam was not there. She checked her cell phone as well as the Capitol phone messages, but found no call from Pam informing of her absence, which was a strict rule of the office. An hour or so passed before Pam returned. Ron Martinez was there to buffer.

"Ah, Tryphena, what a delight to see you." As always, Ron was charming and gracious. "I had stopped by to see if you ladies would be interested in breakfast. Pam was the only one here. We waited a bit and then just went on ahead, as I have things to attend to. I'll be sure to take you to lunch before session is through."

Tryphena could find little reason to protest, and let it go. She was as of yet unaware of the incident from last night. Feeling under the weather with seasonal allergies, she had taken an antihistamine and zonked out. Dothan had called her several times, very late, but had not left a message. Her first order of the day was to find out what was going on. Pam's breakfast with Ron had distracted her. Once in her office, the door closed, she made her call back.

"JD, you got a minute?"

"Uh…yeah…what time is it?" It was obvious that he had just woken up.

"Looks like you called me last night, like around midnight—what's up?"

Dothan explained to her what had happened at the AT&T Center. That he had been drunk and probably made a fool of himself in front of everyone.

After hanging up, she was struck by the coincidence of Pam and Ron's little meal together. *She was acting very smug towards me. Why would Ron take her to breakfast? What is he fishing for? Pam is a rat, I know it. If we are lucky enough to return for next session I won't hire her back. What was the topic of their breakfast I wonder? I know she knows. We all know. Was Judas a member of a circus troop?*

~

That somber evening, Chairman Jackson and Vice Chairman Ron Martinez sat sipping fine scotch in the Cloak Room, a dimly lit enclave of exclusivity and confidentiality next door to the Capitol.

"So Ron, our friend Dothan has been having an affair with Senator Logan. How disgusting. It's only a matter of time before this is discovered. It will destroy everything we've been working for."

"They have to go. We have to get in front of this, Reed. Do you think we should leak it?"

"Of course not. We can't afford this getting out. Besides, what do they know?"

"But they have to go. It's going to get out. This isn't France. Texas is a conservative state. I think we should make a statement explaining our shock and disapproval, informing the public that they have been relieved of their duties. If we instigate this, it will lessen the rotten windfall our way. I personally really like JD, but he has made himself a liability at this point. If they do know anything, they will simply look like disgruntled former employees, so-to-speak. The House version of the bill is the only one that matters, and I'm the author. Logan is irrelevant at this point. I hate to say it, but they are both expendable."

~

Media never sleeps and by morning articles began to circulate in print and online, on blogs and social media, all discussing the Logan-Dothan bill from a new and devastating perspective:

"What's up with Logan and Dothan?"

By lunch it was reported that the two had dated in high school. Their school photographs were everywhere. It was only a matter of days, or even hours, before the dirt would be revealed.

Dothan was visited by the House Speaker and informed of his dismissal from the Select Joint Committee. Rachael's staff discovered this career destroying news while surfing the net. Rachael was now MIA. Dothan, though present on the House floor, was largely invisible.

Collapse could not deter John David Dothan, and he repeatedly tried to contact the Rose of his Memory. Unable to get in touch with her, he sent another poem. *It worked once*, he figured, *maybe it will work again?* As usual he took poetic license:

Is Our Lovemaking a Confessional?

Is our lovemaking a confessional?
You asked me, your head perched on your pillow.
Your creased sheets a pallet of entrails;
Or its thread rifts a trail towards Calvary?

What can I say to you, lying naked?
Does not my nakedness speak for itself?
I am both your green bard sacrificial,
As well as the cursed judge of Judea.

If one exile cannot confide his thoughts,
Plant their futility in the quiet womb
Of his fellow exile; what use this life?
What use this nothingness bereft the void?

If our lovemaking is a confessional,
Then I confess: I confess to its need.
My self-regard absolute; but not so:
Its one flaw, the need of an ear pious.

The poem went without reply.

～

"Did Pro-Life Rachael Logan have an Abortion?" the headline of the *Austin American Statesman* read. Syndicated, the article was all over the planet instantly. This barrage continued, with articles about Dothan's alleged drug use during his rock-and-roll years.

~

Things have a systemic life, with roots reaching into everything. Rachael and her husband separated. But at least her livelihood was her own. Jessica went berserk when the public embarrassment of a philandering husband interfered with her independent lifestyle; Langhorne plain fired Dothan. In district, both a Republican and a Democrat were expressing interest in his House seat.

Dothan refused to relent, sticking it out at the Capitol. Regarding the Immigration Bill, Ron's instinct's proved incorrect. Without Dothan's charisma, it failed to pass on the House floor. Reed Jackson, ever the persevering warrior, refused to be daunted. Several press conferences and meetings with the governor and lieutenant governor were held; a Special Session was in the works.

Regular Session ended with the traditional *Sine Die*. Shortly after adjourning, the governor's proclamation was read on the floor: A Special Legislative Session would convene June 1st. The reason: Three bills: Immigration, Emergency Currency and expansion of the Texas Rangers.

chapter Twenty-one

"Uh yes, can I speak to Mr. John David Dothan please?" A very polite voice asked from the other side of the phone. The voice obviously belonged to a black southern matron.

"Representative Dothan is presently on the House floor, ma'am. Can I take a message?" Tryphnea asked, equally polite.

"Yes could you please tell him that Trudy called from Twin Palms Retirement Home."

"Is there something wrong?" Tryphena inquired.

"I can only talk to Mr. Dothan, young lady. Would you please just tell him that I called?"

Not too shortly there afterward a similar call came in. This time it was Jessica.

"JD is presently on the floor," Tryphena informed her; her voice sparkling with a glint of confidence.

"'JD', huh. Well…well. I think I predicted that one—now didn't I?"

"How can I help you ma'am?" Tryphena asked, impatiently.

"What the hell, I'll just tell you—you can tell him."

"Tell him what?"

"His mother is dead. She passed early this morning, around five a.m."

"Oh my God! That's terrible!"

"She couldn't remember anyone anymore. No one but me, that is. It's for the better."

"When is the funeral?"

"Funeral? That's something JD is going to have to arrange. I won't be there. I would go, but I would have to cancel a trip I've had planned for quite some time. Bad timing I suppose."

Struck by this woman's coldness, Tryphena recoiled, but only briefly. *Perhaps it is better that she won't be present at the funeral. I'm sure I'll get stuck arranging it. He'll be devastated, even if it is for the better. I don't know how much more this man can take?*

Dothan returned from the floor later that afternoon. The Special Session, having only recently gotten underway, although more contentious from a House floor perspective due to the legislation being argued, was for staff far more laid back. For Tryphena, it was lonely as well. Pam had been let go, and the interns were gone. It was now presently like it had started, with just her and JD. *I just hope it doesn't end like it started.* This was a notion that would not leave her be. The freshman Chief of Staff feared that her first tour of duty might be her last. Many of her staff friends up and down the hallway had urged her to quit, as her association with Dothan was too dangerous. But Tryphena refused to abandon her rouge legislator. If she had hitched her wagon to a fallen star, then so be it.

Once Tryphena had informed JD of his mother's passing, she braced herself for a reaction. A monotone Dothan excused himself and quietly made his way back to his private office. The door was not entirely shut, with a healthy fracture visible. Standing cautiously on the other side, Tryphena listened for something, anything. After only silence was offered up to the ether, she left to grab a late lunch.

Tryphena was right; she had the burden of arranging the funeral. It was more than just appalling to her what funeral homes charged…it was plain extortion. One thing she had learned from her brief tenure in the House: businesses were bigger welfare queens than welfare queens.

~

Delilah Dothan was buried in Matagorda County in a plot next to Dothan's father, Phillip. Desperate for money after Phillip had died, some quarter century ago, Delilah had almost sold the plot back to the funeral home. She had ultimately refrained. Dothan was grateful.

Tryphena had accompanied him. The sparse attendees were largely close family and trusted friends. Still Dothan could not help feeling that somehow he had recently dishonored his family name. When the Methodist service was over and the casket was in the ground, Dothan turned from the fresh earth that covered his mother's grave and gazed out at the hazy coastal flats. Summer was here and sweat puddled and ran beneath his suit and dress shirt.

Amidst all of these negatives there existed one positive: The beach house would remain Dothan's residence until the separated couple could negotiate a sale. Years ago, Langhorne had offered to pay the mortgage. Dothan had kindly refused. Now he saw that little piece of self-sacrifice as a stroke of brilliance. The last thing he wanted at this point was to be beholden to his father-in-law regarding his house. The place would yield a healthy profit, half of which would be his.

Dothan got drunk at the funeral reception. He did not make a scene however, his depression so ubiquitous that he merely sulked. Tryphena was relieved to know that even rich white people could have such horrible relatives. She was ready to go almost from the moment they got to the reception hall.

Neither was up for the trip back to Austin. The beach house was the obvious lodging choice. Once on the peninsula, she began to relax; the natural impulse a beach affords the soul. It had been months since she had felt this mellow, if ever.

The two sat up drinking and listening to Dothan's old recordings. Tryphena was impressed and a little startled that the voice careening through the speakers belonged to her boss. *OK, this makes him even more interesting, and explains a lot, too. But how did he ever appeal to an uptight Republican like Rachael Logan?*

At some point, it was time to turn in; Tryphena retired to her room and Dothan to his. Although somewhat hammered, Dothan could not sleep; his thoughts were all over the place. Eventually, they settled around the subject of the women in his life, and how he had fucked things up so badly. Surprisingly, he pondered Jessica first.

What had happened there? Images started to ripple in his head. First he saw him and Jessica, lying wasted on a blanket like two hippies out of time, tripping acid in the summer heat, watching *Othello* at an outdoor theatre. He recalled the clouds over head, the feel of the grass on the flesh of his hand; the feel of Jessica's cool breath, blowing on his hot forehead; the softness of her tongue; his head on the pillow of her breasts. Vividly he remembered lying here in the dark, the feeling of being alive. He knew his longing was cliché. But he could not escape its gravity: A pull, which ironically freed instead of groundeing him, like he was touching down on a foreign planet...*perhaps Bradbury's Mars before the humans?* It all ordered itself so well there in his head.

The image of Rachael fluttered forward obtusely, erasing his previous thoughts. But her memory was so painful; causing the man to shake like a fever had suddenly come on. His analytic mind could not help but unearth every tiny detail of where he had gone wrong. Things he had said, inflections down to the syllable; facial expression and body language.

Had I gotten it all wrong, from the beginning? he wondered. *How could I have misread the world so dramatically?* He could vaguely recall his mother reading him the Romantics when just a child. Although he could not understand it all, the colors that the words evoked were indelible. This memory bled into a recollection of him and his mother sitting at the kitchen table together making Easter eggs; the smell of vinegar always brought this memory back. The world back then oozed possibility. Now all that he desired seemed quite impossible. In elementary school he would win an award for most creative Easter egg. The other children could not grasp this and were naturally jealous of John David. He was made fun of.

Was he born an artist or was he made one? While he had arrived at the creature that he ultimately became, there was no doubt that it was a mistake. *The world wants nothing of art, he thought…nothing. There are no rebels…only artless poseurs. All the beauty and grace, talent and wisdom have gone out of this world. What we are left with is an institutional mediocrity.*

How could I have gotten it all wrong? This world will never arrive at a day of cooperation. It is darkness and more darkness with very little light.

"We kill the light," he muttered into the darkness of the room. The world was not victims and oppressors, but takers and givers; this designation having little to do with class or economics. Yet as much as he scolded, to himself, his socialist brethren, he cursed the likes of Rachael as well. *If Jesus was real,* he thought, *when he returns the very same people that crowd into these churches will be the very same people that pierce his side.*

Everything in his eyes was false.

He was alone now and without a job. All the love in his world had vanished. There were no real friends, nothing. Everything had expired in its own way.

Everything but Tryphena.

The thought of her caused him to discard the bed sheets. Suddenly, he felt hot. Before retiring, he had set the thermostat at 70 degrees. He could hear it kicking on and off. Rising from bed, he reached up to feel the vent. The air blowing was cool. Lying back down, he stared into the blankness. *Tryphena…*

~

Tryphena lay in bed in the guest room just down the hall. Although she had a phobia of spiders and bugs, which she always feared from rooms seldom occupied, she had stripped completely naked before slipping under the sheets. *Why am I naked? Is it because that I know he is near?* Instinct took over in the woman and her sleek fingernails found their way to her inner thighs. How tired she was. Between the hum of the air conditioner and the cadence of the sea, which were audible in intervals, she was gently being lulled to sleep. *I don't have the energy to make myself cum.* But she could not fall asleep. *Where is Rudy? He had so much potential. Is he still working at the restaurant? Why don't the men I like ever seem to have their shit together?*

JD…John David…I think I like John David better. Even when they have it together it's not together. God I hope he hasn't thrown his life away. Goddamn it. I have fallen for another fuck-up…but he's so creative and charismatic and, even though he's insecure, he's confident and vice-versa. I want to go to him. How can I? What can I do? I want to be in his bed.

~

From his bed, Dothan felt his cock getting hard. He remembered the time she had put her hand on his neck; how he had wished she would massage his shoulders. The times he was hit with a waft of her perfume, the warm scent of her breath…

~

Tryphena was sitting on the edge of the mattress. The moisture between her legs both excited and disturbed her. *What am I doing? I need to pee! Maybe I can walk down the hall naked to the bathroom…maybe he'll come out of his room…maybe I'm a fucking idiot.*

Fool or not, inertia lifted her beautiful bare form: the legs leading her to the door; the long slim fingers turning the knob; the pretty two-toned feet padding softly down the hallway carpet. Sitting on the toilet, the cool seat and tile were giving her cold feet. After wiping herself, the wanton dampness had vanished. *He'll reject me…you know he will. He likes rich cowardly white women who disappear and drive him insane. She's so thin. Look at me.* Tryphena, still sitting on the toilet, pinched a bit of flesh from her middle. *What am I thinking? I will lose my job.*

Sneaking ashamedly back to the guest room, she heard something jostle down the hall…

Dothan, in only his underwear, rose from the edge of his bed. He wondered if he could be sued for sexual harassment in his own house. Not that he was intent on pushing himself on his guest, but that he so wished to do so. He knew it was insane, but he wanted to go to her. Standing in the dark at the door of his room, he placed his grip on the handle, while resting his tired head against the door itself.

Tryphena, torn between her need to keep her job and her desire to offer her earthen flesh up to John David, chose the latter. The twenty feet or so from his room to hers seemed endless, with each step a mixture of hope and fear.

Suspended, separated by only an inch of door, the two stood facing one another, unknowingly. For some time the two remained in this position, listening intently for something. Neither heard whatever it was they wished to hear. After some time they returned to bed respectively.

~

"You have absolutely nothing to eat," Tryphena informed Dothan from the den sofa, where she sat Indian-style, sipping a cup of coffee.

"I'm sure. Jessica rarely shops—for food that is," Dothan replied. His long hair was a mess as he had just crawled out of bed.

"I made us some coffee, it's in the kitchen. Wake up sleepy head."

"God, I'm starving," Dothan said, sitting down next to Tryphena.

"Love the hair, I think this is a new look for you, JD."

"It couldn't make things any worse."

"Stop it. Don't you go to negative-town on me."

"I'm starving."

"You said that. Is there any place at all to eat around here?"

"No, we have to get off the peninsula. There's stuff just over the land bridge."

"Well grab a ball cap and let's get out of here."

"Let me finish my coffee."

~

The pair opted for a Waffle House just over the water in Matagorda. Sitting at a booth, they waited for the waitress to take their order.

"I could get used to this coastal life. It's so laid back and with the sea breeze it's not quite as miserable as Houston."

"I wouldn't speak too soon sugar," the haggard waitress interjected.

"I'm sorry?" Tryphena asked confused.

"Sorry for overhearin' and such, but thought I heard you say you could get used to livin' here?"

"Well yes, it's so laid back."

"Not if we get that hurricane."

"What hurricane? Dothan asked.

"Haven't ya'll heard?"

"No, we haven't."

"Yeah, we got a disturbance in the Gulf. They say with the conditions it should be a tropical storm by tomorrow and maybe a hurricane the day after."

"A hurricane from the Gulf in June? That's rare," Dothan added.

"Well yeah, that's what the news has been sayin.'"

"This is what happens when you don't watch TV for a few days," Dothan sarcastically commented, looking at Tryphena. Then turning to the waitress inquired, "What *have* they been saying?"

"Well, it don't look good. They think it will hit the upper Texas Coast. This ain't happened for real since like…1950 something—or so they say."

"Yes, it was Hurricane Aubrey in '57. She was a Cat 4. And one before that, though it was a little later in the summer, it formed in the Gulf too…it only took two days to form I think. It was a Cat 3 and hit near Galveston; both were devastating."

"That's what they've been sayin' on the news, 'devastatin.'" Ya'll folks like to order sumthin?"

chapter Twenty-Two

"Wow, JD, this guy at the *Houston Chronicle* really hates you. He puts your House seat at the top of his list. What an asshole," Tryphena informed a preoccupied Dothan as the two sat idle in his office. The legislature had suspended all activity for the rest of the week due to Hurricane Dante, already a Category 2 storm. It appeared to be rapidly heading for the upper Texas Coast.

"What list is this?"

"The article is titled, 'Ten most vulnerable seats in the Texas Legislature.'"

"I don't know Tryphena, somehow I have a hard time really caring at this point. The bastard sharks can tear the seat to pieces if they wish. As far as I'm concerned, the Texas Legislature is simply not worth it. You make almost no money. You're constantly opening your wallet for this or that. It's a racket for the rich. I'm living on my savings at this point. My beach house is my one cash cow. That's why I have to get down there. Try to batten it down and get my valuables out."

"It's dangerous, JD. Are you sure they won't have the land bridge closed off?"

"I called the County Judge. Of course he didn't return my call, but his assistant called back and told me that the county was leaving the bridge open for the time being."

"What about Jessica?"

"She got most of her shit—at least the stuff she wants—out these last couple of days."

"What are you going to get? Can I help?" Tryphena's tone was growing desperate.

"No, I want you to stay here. I'm going to get my music stuff out; my rare books, the volumes I can't replace; a few family heirlooms, and my writings."

"What about the rain, how are you going to keep it dry in the back of your truck?"

"I have a few tarps. It's not raining yet. I figure I'll have until morning, which is why I'm leaving now."

"Please be careful JD," she implored.

Dothan took off. He had a long drive ahead of him, one made longer by his increasing anxiety. Early George Strait and Merle Haggard had been in his CD player for the last few weeks; The Hag's voice and tales in particular serving as a catharsis. But he was sick of disappointment and heartache. Dothan was bouncing back. In truth, he thought himself too old now for a broken heart. Referencing D.H. Lawrence, he refused to take it tragically. He knew how to suffer incognito; it was like breathing. Once past Bastrop, throwing in The Doors *Strange Days*, he hit the gas and the open road.

~

Not long after Dothan had left the Capitol, Ron Martinez popped-in to his office. "Well hello Tryphena, may I ask how you are holding up?"

"We're hanging in there. I'm really worried that JD is a 'one and done' legislator."

"Yes, I'm sorry for how things have worked out. The chairman was hasty in his decision I believe. Of course I can see his side, as well. I would have handled it differently, I think. If JD is a one termer, I'm sure we can find a place for you somewhere."

"I appreciate that Ron." As usual, Tryphena was smitten by Ron's charm. "Let's hope I don't have to take you up on that."

"So where is JD?" Ron asked, forcibly.

"He's racing back down to the coast."

"Home! You're kidding me. Though I must say I'm not surprised. He had mentioned to me, while on the floor the other day, about how he had some irreplaceable things he was concerned about."

Tryphena, rose from her desk and walked over to the filing cabinet. She was speaking to Ron with her back turned. "I told him to be careful. It would have been pointless to try and persuade him otherwise. I offered to help."

"Well, I'm sure he knows what he's doing."

"Let's hope…"

Upon turning, she discovered Ron had vanished. The front door to the office was wide open. "Ron?" she called, peering out the door and around the hallway. *OK, that was strange.*

But everyone acts strange to me now. It's like I have Ebola or something.

She moved from the front desk to Dothan's office and sat at his computer. It was customary for her to check his emails regularly, both State and private. Very little was on his State email, and as for his private account, mostly mailing lists and spam. One subject line attracted her interest however, the line in question reading, 'Read: Concerning Warren.' It was from an email address she did not recognize. She clicked on it and found only a link to what appeared a news article. Clicking on the link, she was lead to the *Quorum Report* website. And scrolling down, read: Political Guru Warren Jenkins found dead and mutilated in S&M role-play scenario.

"Oh my God!" she cried out loud. Reading the article, she immediately recalled the meeting she and Dothan had had with Warren. The circumstances of the story were so bizarre that it could not possibly be true. *Warren wasn't paranoid. He was murdered: Murdered by the same people that killed Harry Spencer. I have to tell Ron!* She burst into Ron's office and found only his admin.

"…but he was just in our office!" she said, desperately.

"I'm sorry ma'am, but he left abruptly a few minutes ago."

Vacating Ron's office, Tryphena stumbled back in a state of bewilderment. But it was all starting to order itself in her head. *Ron is Vice Chair of the Select Joint Committee. JD's office is next door to Ron's. JD is asked to join the committee the day he and Ron meet. Warren was hired by Reed to take out Harry. JD is let go after Ron's 'breakfast' with Pam. JD's office is next door to Ron's—they've never met! JD ends up on the committee! And the location of Ron's district…oh my God, Harry's letter was true! He just didn't know the whole story! I have to call JD!*

Tryphena hit Dothan's number repeatedly; no one answered. Digging through her House Member contact information she called his home phone. She left a desperate message.

Mired in indecision and panic, Tryphena impulsively decided to brave the storm herself.

~

Dothan was already hitting rain. He obviously miscalculated this storm. A Gulf Coast native, he had developed an instinct for storms. But something like Dante hadn't occurred in almost sixty years.

Although his phone was on, the music that blasted in the cab of the old Ford rendered Tryphena's repeated calls mute.

Now, zooming Matagorda County, the ride was becoming an arduous one.

The land bridge was indeed open, but the wind and rain were so heavy that Dothan's windshield wipers were having trouble keeping up. Before Hurricane Alicia struck in 1983, he remembered sitting with his father on the roof of their well-to-do home. In the distance, a tiny strip of black appeared, and with it a zealous wind. The strip became a band, and then gradually became the sky.

Dothan had left in the late afternoon. It wasn't even seven yet and already it was getting dark. The house appeared.

Luckily the electricity was still on. Jessica had left the out-side lamps lit, which became visible through the rapidity of his struggling wipers. Dothan pulled into the carport and hurriedly withdrew the tarps and rope from behind the old Ford's long, single cab seat.

Once inside, the house was as dead as a burial chamber. First things first: he had been in so much haste that he had forgotten to stop and get beer. He could not recall if there were any in the fridge.

"There is a God after all!" the agnostic stated sarcasti-cally, pulling out a cold one. But a bolt of lightning, a crash of near-by thunder and a flickering of the electricity found him re-calcitrant. "No, really Lord! I am grateful!" he acknowledged, realizing he did not have a flashlight. Fear was coming on. A thunk was heard. Looking out the back windows, he discov-ered, contrary to what Jessica had told him, that she had not had the handyman tie the back balcony furniture down.

He switched on the den's overhead lights and inserted Bob Dylan's *Nashville Skyline*. He plopped down on the floor where his music collection ran the length of several long shelves and began running his fingers over the expanse of re-cord spines...searching. The Alarm, *Declaration* was a keeper. It was an album that had changed his life; *strange how music can do that to some*, he thought. It always amazed Dothan that there were people who had never been moved at all by music, any music. These were people that could not be trusted.

The pile of LPs, 45s, CDs and even cassette tapes, con-tinued to grow: *The Reivers, Dream Syndicate, Rain Parade,* etc.

Dothan's music collection was littered with the obscurely hip and the artistically misunderstood: *Wire Train, Big Country...*

His book collection was even more immense.

He rummaged through the pantry and closets, searching for boxes. In his haste he had come unprepared. Debris scattered the floor as he tossed out contents of drawers and wastepaper baskets.

The doorbell rang.

The doorbell? What? he wondered as he snaked his way to the front door.

"Ron?" he asked, startled.

"JD, man you're here!" Ron said relieved, his cell phone in his hand as if he had been trying to call.

"Have you been trying to call me?"

"Well, yeah. It just goes straight to voicemail. But now I can't even get a signal."

"Shit, it's the storm. We should shut our phones off so the storm doesn't kill the charge."

"Good idea."

"Come in out of this mess."

Ron entered the house. His suit mildly soaked.

"What are you doing here, Ron? What the hell is going on?"

"Tryphena told me you were here. I remember what you had said on the floor. I thought it was the least I could do under the circumstances." Ron answered, looking around the den. "I only have my Lincoln Town Car. Where are you parked? I didn't see your truck."

"Around back in the carport."

"Let's get this show on the road, this is getting nasty fast. This is crazy man."

"Just livin' on the Gulf Coast, comes with the territory, Ron."

"I understand. I'm not that far myself, you know."

"Well, Ron, if you would, just stack those records into that trash can. When it's full or getting too heavy to lift, place it over here by this back door," Dothan said, pointing.

"Right on, JD."

"While you're doing that, I'm going to check my answering machine. I saw the light blinking."

Dothan entered the kitchen. The answering machine, which sat on the counter, was just out of sight from the den where Ron was packing. Dothan hit the 'Play' button with his index finger. Several old messages of no concern ran until he deleted them. Then, the voice of Tryphena came blaring:

"JD, oh my God…listen to me…Warren Jenkins is dead. He's been killed in some bizarre way…I don't know. What I do know is that I think Harry Spencer's letter is true…100%. The only thing is he forgot one culprit, Ron Martinez. That's right, JD…Ron! I think Ron is in this thing with Reed Jackson, has been all along. And listen to this: he came by asking where you were. I'm so fucking stupid I told…"

The message cut off. There was another message indicated on the machine. Dothan felt an electric bolt race up his spine as he fidgeted with the play button and volume. The sound of leather soles echoed closer.

"Ron? What's up?" Dothan asked, peculiarly hunched over the counter.

"What's up? This is what's up." Ron drew an Army Action Colt .45. "I got this from Reed, in case you're wondering."

"I wasn't wondering," Dothan replied, stepping back from the counter. He now stood in the middle of the kitchen. "I am wondering why the fuck you just pulled a gun on me Ron."

"Are you, JD? I wonder. Something tells me that you know very well."

"I have no clue what you are talking about."

"Don't play dumb with me. I know everything."

"Everything?"

"I know that goddamned moron pervert Harry Spencer sent you and Warren Jenkins a letter, spilling the beans."

"The beans?"

"It's true, isn't it?" Ron asked, then distracted, he turned his head towards the den, "You! It's about time."

"Who the fuck are you talking to Ron?"

"None of your business, at least not yet. If you cooperate, and tell me what you know, I'll spare you a death you cannot imagine," Ron stepped back, "Ah hell, why not, I'd like to introduce you to a friend of mine. The Gulf Cartel call him 'Contact.'"

A short, stocky man appeared, dressed in blue jeans, a black t-shirt and an olive dress jacket. He appeared to be Hispanic.

"Do you know why he's called 'Contact?'"

"No," Dothan answered, perplexed.

"…because he puts you in contact with your maker," Ron answered, laughing sardonically. "Now, what do you know?"

"What letter from Harry Spencer?"

"You're not a very good liar, JD. Warren confessed. Of course it took us sticking a knife in his scrawny balls before he confessed, but he did indeed confess. How ridiculous he looked dressed in all that leather," Ron said, grinning.

"What did you sick motherfuckers do to Warren? What did he confess?"

"I already told you, that you received a letter from Harry."

Contact threw open his green overcoat, unsheathed a silver machete, and stepped forward.

"And what of it?"

"You're wondering, I know you are."

"Wondering what?"

"Wondering if it's true," Ron said, smiling insanely.

"If what's true?

"The answer is yes, JD. Yes, *we* had all those children on the school bus destroyed."

"Jesus Christ!"

Contact advanced.

"Contact would like to send him a message on your behalf," Ron joked.

"So you and Reed set all this up?"

"For all practical purposes, yes. There are forces involved here you wouldn't believe, but yes, Reed and I, 'set all this up.'"

"Why? What the hell for? You are a Democrat...your people...you're a Hispanic for Christ's sakes!" Dothan stepped back in response to Contact's continued forward motion.

"You…you white liberals are so smug. 'My people'…what do you know of 'my people.' I'll tell you about my people: Soon we will be the *big* majority. Soon we will have the power. Why answer to some diluted United States that has no moral compass, no rudder. With the equity alone our state has in its possession, Texas could monetize the debt of half the Western world. We've hit the national iceberg. The ship is rapidly sinking. We have the biggest and the best lifeboat. It's time to brave it alone."

"So the succession thing, that's real?"

"What do you think we're doing? Are you that big of a fool?

"It's cold out there you know?"

"It always is, JD." Ron spoke with an air of finality. He then continued, "Reed saw you as only a potential pawn. I pegged you as a sort of visionary, a libertine yes, but a man who could see with the eyes of a poet. I can see I was wrong all along. You are nothing more than a common sentimentalist."

"At least I'm not a murderer of children."

"How feeble you are, falling in love with that slut Rachael Logan. God. I told Reed over and over again what to do and what not to do…but he wouldn't listen. He suffers from the same fatal flaw that all people suffer from who think they are the smartest person in the room."

"And what fatal flaw is that, Ron?"

"They get sloppy. I knew Harry was a liability right away. He should never have been involved at all. But no, Reed is so loyal. So loyal it got Harry killed."

"And me, you sold me down the river, didn't you?"

"You are a good man JD, despite your defects, which are many, but circumstances and your bad judgment have rendered you a liability. At some point I will be more than just a governor, I'll be President. No matter how much I like you, JD, I won't let you fuck that up."

"Let's get this done. This storm is getting bad," Contact finally spoke, his accent heavy.

"I told you never to speak. Never!" Ron scolded.

Dothan appeared trapped in his kitchen, as Ron and Contact guarded the only perceivable entryway/exit. Through the duration of the evening, the electricity had been tenuous, flickering in and out. Now, a bolt of lightning simultaneous with a hammer of thunder and the lights went out!

Black.

Dothan kept his cool. He slipped out the utility door located just off the kitchen. He wondered if his boots could be heard rumbling down the wooden steps. It took seemingly an eternity to reinstate the device, but with his cell phone finally on, its screen light illuminated enough of the garage.

Ron and Contact were in a state of confusion: blind in a foreign environment. Dothan could hear the two arguing up above, although he could not make out what it was they were saying. Grabbing a sharpshooter shovel from the wall where it hung, he made his way to the carport where the trusty old Ford sat. The tires were slashed.

The electricity clicked back on!

With the sharpshooter in hand, Dothan tried negotiating the pouring rain. But the lights again flickered and then died.

"JD, where are you going, my friend?" Ron hollered. He was now outside. "Maybe we should call it a night and head back to Austin…find that pretty Chief of Staff of yours. Contact's getting hungry!"

With the wind and the rain and the darkness it was impossible to navigate more than a few feet at a time. The storm surge was flooding under the beams that supported his house. Hurricane Dante was making landfall at this very instant! Dothan stood paralyzed not knowing what to do.

"Maybe Contact will have his way, please her with his blade! And what of your lady friend, Rachael? Contact's getting hungry!"

Staring into the lashing void, the shamed Representative of House District 100 had a choice: He could run, perhaps make his way back to the mainland before the storm claimed him. But Dothan had had enough of this sick fuck and the trained animal he kept on a leash. He had lived here for fifteen years. He could navigate the house and grounds if he were deprived of all his senses.

Ron's voice approximated the back deck.

Dothan's cell phone was still glowing, despite the downpour. Towards the back balcony, he steadily wound his way through the landscaping, which whipped like a serpent. A rotating circle of light was observed. Ron and Contact had a flashlight!

Hurricane Dante was hitting Matagorda Peninsula as a Category 3 storm; several hours ahead of schedule.

Sand and palm tree particles flew through the air like hail. Ron and Contact were currently standing above Dothan, just as he thought, on the back deck. Dothan stood below in three feet of powerful, undulating water. His phone was no longer working. Inching towards the stairs leading to the porch, he made his way nearly blind. A window shattered; then another and another.

"JD!" Ron shouted into the rotating chaos. "JD!"

"He's gone! The storm took him!" Contact yelled, bracing himself against the balcony rail. "It's getting hard to stand! Let's take shelter!" the killer pleaded.

Ron turned from where he stood. Over and over he made a frantic circle, trying to ascertain the situation. He was met with the sharp edge of a shovel to the neck and shoulder!

"EEEAHH!" Ron screeched in pain and surprise; his shriek competing with the yell of the wind. Ron dropped, hitting the wooden planks. His eye and right hand still literate, he fired the .45!

An odd fire burned in Dothan's abdomen. A phase of nothingness swept his right side. From the deck floor he squinted and gaged. A loud crack broke the bellow of the circular wisp. One of two large palm trees, towering above the deck, collapsed. Contact dropped like a condemned man from the gallows. Water and jagged debris thrashed, tearing him under.

chapter Twenty-Three

For several days, Matagorda Peninsula was gone, completely submerged under water. Although she had made haste in her pursuit, Tryphena was unable to make it actually onto the peninsula. But until her boss was found, dead or alive, she was committed to braving the aftermath; lodging in one of the only available motel rooms with running water in Bay City, the county seat of Matagorda. FEMA agents were everywhere, as were the National Guard. Trailers littered the devastated landscape. This was an unmitigated disaster. The young Chief of Staff found it all surreal.

Wandering the cleanup and rescue site, Tryphena would ask repeatedly of whatever official or officer who might listen, "Has anyone found Representative Dothan?" She would also inquire if there were any signs of Representative Ron Martinez.

"No," was the answer to both.

Regarding Ron, it was presumed that he had been present when the storm hit because his El Dorado had been discovered in the quickly receding water.

The Coast Guard found Representative John David Dothan unconscious atop a piece of floating siding; presumably ripped from his now vanished home. Dothan was Life-Flighted to Houston, which had sat on the dirty side of the storm, but had fared remarkably well. Tryphena rode with him.

No sign of Ron. Nothing at all.

Tryphena sat in the hospital waiting room, her hair and clothes filthy. Some sixteen hours earlier, she had been informed of Dothan's condition.

The doctor spoke to her, although he was breaking protocol. "We have been unable to reach his wife, but as he is a State official, and you are his top person, I'm going to inform you of his status even though it is customary to notify the next of kin before anyone else."

"How is he? Please tell me he's going to make it," Tryphena pleaded.

"He has a gunshot wound to the abdomen. We have not yet removed the bullet. There is an infection in his small intestine. We're treating it with antibiotics, but when we remove the bullet, we may have to perform surgery to remove a portion of his small intestine."

"Oh my God! Why haven't you removed the bullet?"

"Actually that's the least of our worries. Mr. Dothan has suffered a stroke…"

"Oh my God!"

"It's a relatively small stroke, only four millimeters on the left side of his brain. However, because of the circumstances, since this likely happened days ago, the damage is disproportionate to what it would have been under normal circumstances."

"What are you saying?"

"We're not certain, because he is still unconscious, but we believe the right side of his body may have been adversely affected. How much, we can't say."

"You mean he may be partially paralyzed?"

"Yes ma'am. The reason we haven't removed the bullet is because of this reality. His blood pressure has finally stabilized, so that's good. We're doing everything we can do at this time."

"Why is he unconscious?"

"The stroke, combined with the gunshot wound, as well as the event he has just endured. He is most likely in a state of shock."

"But he will…"

"It is my firm belief he will come out of it. In what condition is obviously the question that concerns us the most at this time."

"When might we know?"

"That I can't say, but, being a State official, he will get the best care available."

Tryphena was left alone to ponder her confusion in the bleak waiting room. Needing the bathroom, she moped down the hospital hallway to her destination. Standing before a most unflattering mirror, she lifted her stinking T-shirt, which reflected a bony rib cage. *Well I've wanted to lose weight forever it seems. Be careful what you wish for.*

She crashed her tired butt down on one of the waiting room chairs and as she did, the large flat screen that hung on the wall in a corner of the waiting area caught her attention. It was a picture of Reed Jackson, his ugly old mug the width of the screen.

Tryphena rose from her chair and walked toward the respective corner. "Excuse me," she asked, raising her voice to a hospital worker who sat behind the information desk some thirty feet away. "Yes, ma'am…can you help me here? I need to turn this up, now!"

The ugly mug of Reed was luckily just a prelude of what was coming after the commercial break. With the volume up, the talking head looked her straight in the eye and reported: "…State Senator Reed Jackson was arrested by the FBI today and charged with numerous felonies, not the least of which is Conspiracy to Overthrow the Government. In a plot that is now only just beginning to be unveiled, it is alleged that Senator Jackson was instrumental in last fall's school bus bombing in South Texas that claimed the lives of everyone on board. This act of terrorism, initially attributed to the drug cartels as retaliation to the federal government's recent passing of a comprehensive immigration law, is now allegedly the work of Senator Jackson and possibly numerous others yet to be disclosed. A source, which at this point remains anonymous, tipped the Feds off after the brutal murder of political consultant Warren Jenkins. Jenkins' murder was preceded by the apparent suicide of former State Representative Harry Spencer. Representative Spencer's death is being reinvestigated, and may be related to

Warren Jenkins' death. We will keep you up to date as this bizarre story unfolds…. As a side note to Reed Jackson, it has been reported by the AP that the State Senator is suffering from terminal cancer…"

~

The story morphed into the missing Ron Martinez and Tryphena's boss. There was no mention of Ron's possible involvement. It ended with clips of the Governor, Lt. Governor and the House Speaker collectively expressing their shock and ignorance. *It's amazing what you miss when you don't have access to technology for a few days*, she thought.

~

Tryphena was running out of money. She could no longer afford to live in motels. Economics demanded she return to Austin and the apartment she was still paying for. There wasn't much to do up at the Capitol as the Special Session had been cut short. The legislation had died. It was *Sine Die* for good.

The FBI and Homeland Security visited the Chief of Staff in her office by. She told them what she knew.

Dothan came out of his coma shortly after her return to Austin. This report was discovered online. Tryphena was broke and wondered how she could make it down to Houston. She would not receive her pay until the first of July. That was several days from now. Self-doubt and insecurity plagued her. *Maybe Jessica is back. Maybe that's a good thing. That doctor acted like he was lowering himself just talking to me. You would think the hospital would call if I were the only one available. Lord please let him be OK. Forgive him his vanity. He is a good man and… I love him.*

Tryphena stayed up waiting for midnight July 1st to strike. With her paycheck deposited, her bags ready to go, she left for the Bayou City.

Dothan had been moved from the ICU to a private room. Although this was a good sign, he was not yet in good enough condition to receive visitors. Tryphena pleaded with the nurses to give her an update. None would.

"Has his wife been found?" she asked in an attempt at understanding their silence.

"No ma'am, you're the only person who has been to see him. It's terrible that no family is here. I'm told he's someone of importance."

The long, hot, humid days hung like a sweaty undergarment. Tryphena hated the summers in Texas, particularly here on the coast. Among her traveling things was her laptop. It was the only device she had to pass the time at the hospital. Frequently, she would login to Cap Web to check email, etc. Dothan had given her passwords to just about every account in his life, including his personal email. Tryphena had largely refrained from logging into it, partly out of guilt and partly out of decency. Recently, although she still experienced the former, she violated the latter. Now, what she found in his inbox brought everything into focus. It was from that same email she did not recognize from before; the address that had alerted her to Warren's death. The address: CarsonKitty... Tryphena opened the email. She read:

Dear John David,

By the time you read this it will most likely be sometime after I have written it. I want you to know that I have prayed for your recovery every day and night. I have asked the Lord to forgive you for your agnosticism, and trust that He will, as you are a good person. Kindness runs through your blood and your soul. Your concern for Carson is a perfect example. (By the way, I have adopted him. He is sitting on the desk as I write this. He says hello.)

I want you to know, that though it is impossible for us to ever be together again, I do love you. You are the love of my life. I am sorry for all that has happened. And I am sorry for not coming to see you. I would have, but it will just cause more nonsense, inhibiting your recovery. This is a vile world we live in, one filled with so much inhumanity; people's obsession with other people's lives perhaps being one of its worst expressions. Know that you are in my thoughts and prayers.

It is I who blew the conspiracy open. Yes, I. Remember the letter you received from Harry? I received a letter as well—I presume a duplicate of yours. I discovered it shortly after I had broken off our affair. (I'm so irresponsible about opening my snail mail.

It was sent when your letter was sent.) I too thought it paranoia, but after Warren was killed I contacted Homeland Security. What ensues from here is anyone's guess.

My term is up next cycle. I will not be seeking reelection. In fact, I have thought about resigning. The Republican Party has abandoned me. After all of the work I have done on behalf of their platform they now want nothing to do with me. So be it.

I will be in touch at some point. I want you to remember John David: Just because I'm not present does not mean that I am absent.

Love forever,

Rachael

Tryphena found herself, in a state of shock; unable to move or speak. Instinctively, she moved the mouse over 'delete'. She was eager to 'right click,' but hesitated. Removing her hands from the laptop entirely, she placed them at her side. She looked at the screen empathetically; the device sitting independently on her tightly closed thighs. *What the hell, Rachael finally made herself useful I suppose. She says that it's impossible to ever be with John David again. Good. Bitch better leave my man alone.*

Tryphena did not delete the email, but instead closed out of the account; resigned to never enter it again.

She sat for some time just daydreaming.

"Ms. Taylor?" the nurse asked, suddenly appearing; her Nigerian accent thick and difficult to make out.

"Yes?" Tryphena replied, startled away from castles she was building in the air, feared the worse.

"Mr. Dothan can see you now, if you like."

"Really, is he OK…I mean can he think and talk? By the way, he's actually Representative Dothan."

"Oh, I'm sorry."

"No problem, just clarifying. So he can see people—finally?"

"Well, yes ma'am. He asked for you actually. And, I don't quite understand, but he wants to hear a song called, "King-a-Pain?"

"Yes, that's the Police!"

"The Police?"

"Yes, that's the band that sings the song, 'King of Pain.'"

"Oh, OK, I thought he wanted me to call the police."

"No. Definitely not. Please do not call the police."

Tryphena was ecstatic. For two weeks she had waited for this moment. It was literally the longest two weeks of her life. Searching the web on her laptop she found a track of "King of Pain." Preparing the song to play, she followed the nurse down the long hall to John David's room.

"Mr. Dothan…?" the nurse asked, opening the respective door.

"Representative Dothan," Tryphena corrected her from behind.

"Yes, I'm sorry, Representative Dothan…Ms. Taylor is here to see you, sir."

"Well, hello John David…"

SINE DIE

About the Author

Matt Minor presently serves as a Chief of Staff in the Texas House of Representatives. He has worked as a political campaign manager and is a well-regarded public speaker. Matt has authored official state publications, oversees syndicated editorials, is a speechwriter and district radio legislative commentator.

Prior to his life in state politics Matt was a professional musician and entertainer; his numerous recordings receiving wide critical praise. Matt practices numerous other arts including the craft of poetry; an interest that has brought academic recognition.

Matt Minor lives with his wife Stacy on their ranch property in Wharton County, Texas. He maintains an apartment in Austin.